More Riverdale Stories

It Happened in Riverdale, Volume 7

Juliana Harvard

Published by Juliana Harvard, 2021.

MORE RIVERDALE STORIES

First edition. June 4, 2021.

ISBN: 979-8201898854

Written by Juliana Harvard.

Also by Juliana Harvard

It Happened in Riverdale
It Happened in Riverdale
November Rain
That Morgan Boy
Beach City Breakup
Escape From Fate
"Marvelous"
More Riverdale Stories

To Riverdale Valley for your golden pink sunsets, rugged mountains, and silhouetted palm trees

"Men! They're All Alike!"

This short story, while using names of specific established characters, seems to be based more on a universal truth expressed in the art of fiction rather than on actual events in time. Stylistically, it is placed among Julie's earlier writing.

"OH, MEN! THEY'RE ALL alike!" These emphatic words came from the lips of a vivacious but frustrated blonde as she bounded into the apartment and flung the door shut with a resounding slam that echoed through the walls of the empty room. In an instant, there appeared from an adjoining room a sleepy little brunette in pin curls and bathrobe.

"Well, good morning," she said. "What's your problem now?"

The other girl forced a smile. "Well, it's not my fault it's 2 a.m. You know Matt. Anyway—" But she stopped.

"Anyway, what?"

"Nothing. Forget it."

Carolyn looked at the youthful figure clad in the blue formal she had purchased just a week ago and the wilted orchid drooping from her shoulder.

"Okay, Gloria," Carolyn sighed. "What happened between you and Matt?"

Gloria hung her head. "Oh," she sputtered, "he just doesn't understand the dignity of a college girl, and he cracked silly jokes all the time at the party. And then when he had to usher in Sunday morning at

Prospect Point—that did it! He acted so childishly, and we didn't have a bit of fun."

"Well, you must remember," Carolyn tried to sympathize, "that Matt is fourteen months younger than you are. You knew that before you started going with him, but you said it didn't matter."

"I didn't think it did then," Gloria admitted, "but believe me," and she shook her head, "I'm through with men—for good!"

Carolyn laughed unbelievingly. But Gloria, ignoring her, went to bed.

The days passed. Gloria and Matt broke up. As Carolyn expected, Gloria soon met another "dream." His name was Ken—tall, handsome, and 24—and came from Carolyn's hometown.

Gloria came in one day on Cloud Nine and almost tripped over the lamp by the sofa. Carolyn, watching from the kitchen, knew something was up. Gloria flung her books onto the floor, flopped into the big old easy chair, and announced dreamily, "I've got a date with a fabulous Marine tonight."

Carolyn sighed. "Who is it?" she asked as a matter of routine.

The stars came out in Gloria's eyes and she sighed, "Ken Nelson," then she told Carolyn all about him.

"Oh, Gloria, hon," Carolyn said, "I know what Ken's really like—we went to school together—and he just isn't your type. He's a big playboy; he's got one in every port."

But Gloria, starry-eyed and lightheaded, wouldn't listen. "You don't know what he's like now. He's different, so much more mature than Matt. You just don't know," she would say. "He's different!"

"He's different." That's the way it always was; that's what Gloria had said every time.

"Okay," Carolyn said out loud. "But don't say I didn't warn you."

So, every night at eight sharp Ken phoned, and every Saturday night—Carolyn could count on it—Ken and Gloria went someplace together. And as the weeks passed, their friendship grew steadily stronger. But it wasn't all "kid stuff" that Gloria talked about, Carolyn noticed. Gloria seemed to be pretty levelheaded and serious about this guy. Carolyn thought maybe she was wrong for once. At least Ken was making more progress than Matt or Tom or Harry or anyone else who had ever gone with Gloria. But then, it was about time Gloria settled down. And the more Gloria talked, Carolyn was just about convinced that this time it was for good.

Then one day Carolyn heard rumors that Gloria and Ken were fighting and almost ready to call it quits. Carolyn couldn't quite believe this nonsense about her best friend. Gloria had said nothing to her; but, of course, Gloria wouldn't say anything. And Ken *did* have a hot temper....

So, Carolyn simply waited and watched. Lately, Gloria didn't seem to be nearly as excited about the whole affair as she first was. No more hitting the ceiling when the phone rang, no more long unlimited chatter about Ken late at night when Carolyn was trying to sleep, no more little girlish squeals of delight when Gloria was relating to Carolyn all the details of a date. Gloria didn't seem to be unhappy, however; but a quiet happiness was new to Gloria's makeup. Should Carolyn be suspicious to think that maybe Gloria and Ken were calling it quits? Or was she just being naïve to believe that Gloria had settled down and learned to control her emotions of what she thought was love?

Then one Saturday night the inevitable happened. Carolyn came home early—around eight-thirty—and both girls were very startled to see each other. Gloria was startled because Carolyn was supposed to work until ten, and Carolyn was startled to even find Gloria home at this hour on a Saturday night. And she wasn't even getting ready to go out. There she sat in her robe curled up in the big chair with a magazine in her hand and a box of chocolates by her side—the last box of chocolates that Ken would ever give her. Carolyn almost knew what was wrong—she spied a wadded tissue on the floor behind the chair.

"Is Ken—ill?" Carolyn asked gingerly.

"No," was the sulky reply.

"Then he's out of town?"

Gloria shook her head. "Can't you guess?" she said sarcastically.

"Well," drawled Carolyn, "I've heard a few rumors—"

"Well, you heard right! Ooh, he just flew off the handle simply because I walked two little blocks from the malt shop with Jim Donaldson. And I've seen him plenty of times with Ella or Sandra or Sarah—and I was dumb enough to believe that they trapped him. Brother! He's so selfish and...and childish! It's a good thing I found out now."

Carolyn could have said a lot of things. Her mind went back to a night many months ago when she had heard the words from those same lips: "Ken's so mature." "Ken's different."

Carolyn could only smile sympathetically while in her heart she thought, "Well, Gloria dear, maybe someday you'll learn—maybe someday."

Just then Gloria sprang to her feet, flung her magazine aside, and just before she disappeared into her room, she repeated those same old familiar words: "Oh, men!" she exclaimed. "They're all alike!"

The Christmas Rainbow

This six-part story is a sequel to "November Rain" when Julie and Allen first fell in love. Sandra tries to help Julie "live in the moment" and to express appreciation for all kinds of love. Original story written by Julie Scott, Christmas 1961. Epilogue written by Juliana Scott Davidson, Christmas 1967. She will become Juliana Harvard six years later, in 1973. The author wrote the "Riverdale" stories in an era when the word "gay" meant "happy" and "joyful." Nothing more.

PART 1. HOLLY LEAVES

The girl had a funny feeling in the pit of her stomach. She couldn't explain it, but it was there. And she sat silently in the winter twilight, staring into the fading sunset. A yellow leaf floated downward and settled at her feet. She looked at it for a long moment, and then she suddenly closed her eyes and shivered in the evening's coolness.

"Oh, come on, Julie!" said someone with a merry voice behind her. "Snap out of it!" Julie felt a hand on her shoulder. She looked up into the face of her lifelong friend, Sandra Lee.

Julie chuckled a bit as she mumbled, "Oh, it's you, Sandra."

"Listen, Juliana Scott, someday you're going to have to learn, like I did, that you can't chase rainbows all your life. Take it from the 'voice of experience.'" She coughed mockingly.

Julie laughed, but Sandra's words somewhat surprised her. Sandra seldom spoke with such sternness.

"Oh, look." Sandra sat down on the loveseat beside Julie. "Pretend I'm Allen," she said, putting her arm on the back of the seat and snuggling up close like Allen might have done at one time.

Julie sat up straight. "Phooey on Allen!" she sputtered with total disgust. "Who needs him?"

Sandra jumped to her feet and pulled Julie up with her. "Good! I've got you out of your mood now. Let's go get ready for the party!"

So, casting aside her sunset and falling leaves, Julie followed Sandra to her room.

Julie watched her friend vigorously brushing her hair and chatting pleasantly in anticipation of the coming party. *How can she be so gay?* Julie thought. *She's my best friend, and even she can't understand how I feel.*

"Don't you think Kurt's neat?" "Hey, did I tell you Allen called me last night?" "Man, that Steve! You know he wanted to *take* me tonight?" "Oh, yes, I got a letter from LeRoy today." "Raymond's coming home from college week after next! Isn't that fabulous?" "I saw Ken downtown Thursday. You know, he doesn't 'get' me as much anymore." "Say, I hear Jim is home. Do you think he'll be there tonight?" These were the snatches of chatter Julie caught as Sandra dressed and primped.

Suddenly, Sandra stopped and looked at her friend Julie. "Pep up, Julie!" she exclaimed. "We're going to have a blast tonight, aren't we?" she teased.

Julie knew well what Sandra meant, but she smiled and shook her head. "No, Sandra, not me, not tonight."

"Sure, you will. Wait and see," Sandra said gaily. "Hey, it's almost seven! Let's go!" She picked up two coats, threw one at Julie, and headed for the door.

As Julie got into Sandra's car, she spied something on the floor. "Holly leaves?" she queried, picking up the shapes of green construction paper.

"Oh," replied Sandra, "those must have fallen out of the sack of Christmas decorations Marsha helped me make for Home Ec."

Christmas...holly.... All at once Julie, in a momentary trance, realized why the mood was there as she had watched the sunset and the falling yellow leaf....

PART 2. A CHRISTMAS Party

It *was* a lovely party, although it was very informal, for Mrs. Emory had planned it only a couple of days in advance. The food was superb, and now the kids played ping pong and Chinese checkers. But it got too dull for Sandra and Diana, a vivacious blonde. Well, Steve had his car, didn't he? And Snackies was still open.

Julie observed with interest the various personalities of her teenage friends. There were the younger ones, the 13- and 14-year-olds: chubby, jolly Donald, and Andy with the crew cut, who played ping pong now. There was shy, quiet, but always fun-loving Janette; timid, easy-to-get-along-with Darlene; Darlene's cousin Irene with the mysteriously bewitching eyes. There was the freckle-faced mischievous Frank, Ella's little brother, who was now "goofing off" with his Mexican friend Carlos just home from boarding school. Sam and romantically smiling Alice sat in a corner with another couple, the new guy Joe and pretty, blonde, but socially insecure Samantha. She admired very much the boy beside her who strummed the guitar. Then there was the pretty Spanish doll, Margarita, affectionately called Riti. Now she sat talking to Allen—good-looking, witty, and magically charming Allen Macintosh.

The room grew stuffy. Quickly Julie ran from the building, out into the cool night. She did not mind the soft drizzle of rain that fell onto her hair.

In a luxurious white sedan sat the unhappy Steve-chasing Cynthia. Julie watched as Carolyn literally dragged Cynthia out of Steve's car. Then Carolyn climbed in with Steve, and with Sandra and Kurt—an intellectual, but deliciously cute. They invited Julie to go along for the ride. It was short and simple, but fun. The night wore on.

Julie found herself inside once more. Jim, the gay sophisticate who had come to the party only to bring his sister Cynthia, sat playing "Chopsticks" with Allen. Now Allen called Julie to the piano, and she came like a robot.

"Jingle bells, jingle bells..." "Si-i-lent night, ho-o-ly night..." "I'm dreaming of a white Christmas, just like the ones I used to know..." sang the voices of those gathered around the piano, and Julie's hands followed mechanically. Finally, when all had lost interest except Allen, Joe, and Samantha, Allen said, "Play this." He placed music in front of Julie.

"The First Noel." The rickety old piano in the empty hall sounded sick, but Allen stood by its side, completely entranced. When Julie had finished, he said, "Play it again, please?"

Julie looked at him in wonder. There was a faraway look in his eyes and a strange glow on his face. Julie caught the spell—the atmosphere, the breath of Christmas.

"I like it," he said, looking down at her. And Julie played it again.

"Anyone need a ride home?" Sandra called as she flew down the steps. "I've got Daddy's car tonight."

"I do," Allen called back. Then, "Is it all right, Mom?"

Mrs. Macintosh hesitated. "Okay. But eleven o'clock and not one minute later!"

Kurt, naturally, sat in the front beside his sweet Sandra; so Allen climbed into the back beside Julie. The night was chilly, and their warmth breath collected on the inside of the windows. Julie remembered another night, almost a year ago, when another car had been "fogged up." It had been soon after last year's Christmas. But instead of Kurt and Sandra, there had been another couple, Ken and Gloria. Then, a touch of a hand and a look in two sincere blue eyes was all it took to write an innocent love. Now, the warmth of Allen's arms felt pleasant to Julie;

but, like the spring violets frozen in the ground, she was numb, feeling no emotion for the boy whose lips pressed close against her own....

"Sure, it's going to be fun! Don't you think so?" Sandra couldn't understand Julie. She turned off the engine of the car as they pulled into Julie's driveway.

Julie forced a smile and laughed nervously. "Yeah. It'll be great."

"Then why are you acting so scared?"

"Sandra," Julie sighed, "I was there *last* year."

"With Allen," Sandra added with an air of finality.

PART 3. REMEMBERING Mexico

Christmas in Mexico! Last year it was an adventure; this year, well, Julie didn't know. There would be the same little town, the same old Spanish school, and probably most of the same young people—but not the same Allen.

Only a year ago, a very happy boy and girl were going to all the meetings together that weekend, enjoying each other's friendship, sharing the same faith, and loving the same God. There had been the grassy tree-shaded plaza where they ate in the twilight 'neath the southern stars—the Saturday night walk and the old Spanish mansion and the strumming of a lone guitar. Then there was that Sunday and shopping in Mexico—the scheme of Gloria and Julie to get Allen a real Mexican wallet for Christmas, which was so carefully planned, then so promptly figured out by Allen. Even now, Julie couldn't quite forget the strains of the Spanish chorus fading into the night.

"Romantic, festive, yes; but Christmas isn't *all* built around Allen," reminded Sandra.

"No, not all," agreed Julie. "But he sure helped!"

The old Christmas carols, the simple Christmas story, another log in the stone fireplace—this had been Julie's Christmas Eve last year. That was the night Allen had squeezed her hand so gently and meaningfully, and said, "You're the greatest, Julie. I love you, punkin." That was the night he gave her the white Bible, the symbol of everything good and beautiful, everything their love stood for.

"I know Christmases can be neat," Sandra said now reminiscently. "I remember last year and Christmas shopping with LeRoy..." Then her tone changed suddenly. "But really, men aren't so important. If every Christmas were just exactly alike, it would get pretty boring, wouldn't it? Just forget Allen and have a nice Christmas with your own family! Next year" —and she changed back to the old Sandra again— "who knows? There might be this tall, handsome guy—"

"Allen!" Julie broke in almost teasingly.

"Never can tell!" Sandra laughed as Julie opened the car door. "Goodnight, Julie!" she called as Julie waved from her front porch.

PART 4. CHRISTMAS MEMORIES

Thus, the weekend passed, and Julie was at school again. The December sun shone through the crispy cold air into the windows of the old classroom, which was now quiet as the students finished the English exam. Julie finished; she was rechecking her paper. Then, through the stillness of the afternoon, she heard distant music. The pencil fell into her lap, and she listened. It was a pretty melody—a Christmas song, she knew, but what was the name of it?

Her eyes wandered around the room, and her gaze fell on algebraic figures scrawled on the blackboard and came to rest on an empty desk near the front. It reminded her of a similar desk where Casey had sat in another algebra class *two* years ago. Suddenly she remembered the song— "Sleigh Bells," of course! She saw an assembly gathered and there was Casey, dear Casey, in the school chorus. Julie felt that stuffy warmness of the assembly room and smelled the apple-nut-and-candy packages that the faculty members passed out to the students. The Christmas program had been good, and Casey was especially nice. There were the memories she had of Christmas of her first year in the big high school.

"Be sure your name is on your paper," said Mr. Wesley. "Fold your papers and pass them in." The music faded away and broke the spell. Julie glanced quickly over her answers again, and then the bell rang.

"Hark, the herald angels sing!" rang out through the clear frosty night as the solicitors went from door to door "on behalf of worldwide missions" and bringing Christmas cheer to each home. It gave Julie a warm feeling inside to know she was doing something good for others.

The stars twinkled high above the quiet brown hillside. In her mind, Julie could see a large, brilliant star, and way in the distance a crude little stable where a Babe slept in a manger. She saw the humble kneeling shepherds and the virgin mother with gladness in her heart.

"Julie," a fellow solicitor called, "Mrs. Donaldson said to finish this street down to Arcene Road, and then we'll go back."

"Thank you." Julie took the literature and started on. Many of the solicitors went in two's, but Julie was alone. Not so the Julie of *three* years ago. Then it was Billy Kingston—blond, blue-eyed husky Billy. He was a tomboy gentleman, a ladies' man. There was just something about that Kingston family.

Now Julie rang a doorbell and waited for an answer....

There were merry voices and the sound of laughter as Julie and Sandra and Kurt and Allen approached another house. Someone welcomed them warmly and ushered them into the living room, where Pat Boone records spun on the hi-fi. Julie felt like a puppet, pulled along with the crowd. Soon she found herself in the kitchen by the table, covered with cookies and punch. Mrs. Donaldson was so nice to treat the teenagers who gave their time on a Saturday night. The drink was refreshing, and the cookies were good.

Christmas cookies. Billy and Julie had baked Christmas cookies together. The Kingston kitchen was small, and the aromas were delightful. And Billy's mom Norma was so sweet. Julie had spent many a day with the Kingstons—Norma, Billy, and his brother Eddy. Yes, there *was* something about that Kingston family....

"Well, if you've got to be home by eleven, we'd better be going," Sandra's voice broke into Julie's thoughts. "Thanks for everything, Mrs. Donaldson."

"Yes, thank you," echoed Julie. Numbly, she rose from her chair and headed for the door.

"Julie, what *is* wrong with you?" Sandra almost demanded as they worked on Christmas decorations the next day. "You've been acting so strange."

"Well," Julie's weak voice replied, "maybe it's just Christmas."

"Christmas!" Sandra looked at Julie as if she held in doubt her complete sanity.

"Well, I was just thinking of grade school and Eddy Kingston. Remember how we used to decorate the schoolroom windows? And we drew names to exchange presents. And we'd always gather in Miss Blossom's room and sing Christmas carols from those books we all got for a quarter at Sprouse-Reitz."

Sandra softened and smiled. "Yes, those *were* the good old days." In her mind, she could see the paper wreaths and candles made by childish hands and taped to frosty windows. She heard young merry voices, somewhat off key, and smelled the dampness of those week-before-Christmas mornings. "But," she frowned, "why should memories of happy times make you so gloomy?"

"Oh, I'm not gloomy, exactly," replied Julie. "It's just that with every Christmas tree I smell, every song I hear, every bit of Christmas glitter I see, I relive a Christmas of the past."

"Well, now, you just stop living Christmases past and start living this present Christmas, maybe a simple one with your family, like I said before, you rainbow-chaser." Sandra spoke firmly but not unkindly.

"All the relatives and confusion and noise—the Christmas wrappings all over the living room and dirty dishes all over the kitchen—you call that a *simple* Christmas with my family?"

Sandra sighed then said despairingly, "Okay, so 'family' is out."

"Oh, I'm sorry," said Julie. "I didn't mean to be so pessimistic. Let's get back to work on these decorations."

Sandra's smile was warm and understanding. "You know," she said as they traced and cut, "I think this banquet's going to be neat, don't you? Sure is too bad Kurt can't come. Do you really think Jim Donaldson will ask me?"

"Leave it all to Cynthia Donaldson," Julie assured her. "*You* don't have to worry!"

"Don't you think Allen will ask you?"

Julie shook her head. "The only thing that's stopping him from taking that Sylvia Hawkins is the thirty miles between them. He'll probably end up going with Riti." She shrugged, but deep inside she could not forget.

Sylvia Hawkins! How had *she* come into the picture, anyhow? One minute she was an insignificant unpopular sophomore; the next, a capricious flirt, pursuing and being pursued by the fabulous Allen Macintosh. And Riti—what right did *she* have to Allen, anyway?

Suddenly a hoarse rumble broke the quiet, monotonous sound of snipping scissors. The house quivered, and the sky split in two. Then watery fingers of rain tapped on the windowpane.

"Hey, it's raining!" exclaimed Julie.

"No kidding," was Sandra's nonchalant reply. Then, "Ooh! I've got to get home. Mother and Daddy aren't home, and the washing's on the line and the lawn furniture's uncovered. I'll see you tomorrow, okay?"

Julie watched Sandra run down the wet walk and dive into her car. For a long time, she stood by the screen door, watching. "Rain," she muttered. "Why can't it be snow?"

PART 5. FINDING CHRISTMAS Love

The sun hid behind the clouds, distinct shadows disappeared, and all was a world of gray. Sense of time seemed to slip, slip away. And the rain dropped, dropped, dropped.

And suddenly, out of the gray, gray troposphere, written on every cloud, proclaimed by every droplet, the letters appeared: "L-O-V-E." It was strange that implications of something so good and beautiful and happy should come during such a dreary day and the gloominess that permeated the air. *Mockery*, thought Julie bitterly, *sheer mockery. Is there such a thing as love? What is love? Was it that mutual attraction Julie and Allen once shared?*

"Love," she grunted half aloud. "What does *that* have to do with now—with this Christmastime? Allen doesn't love me—" Suddenly she stopped as she thought emphatically, *So what?!*

The ground shook as the thunder roared and the lightning streaked across the sky. Torrents broke loose from the angry black clouds. But Julie's new concept of love did not fade. Through the rumble and rush, Julie growingly felt the spirit of Christmas—the spirit of love. There was Momma's love for the family in the big, big Christmas dinner she always fixed, Miss Blossom's love in listening to off-key carols and letting schoolroom windows get cluttered with childish decorations, love in the gifts—love in the lovely white Bible from Allen... There were always the pretty cards and festive packages, holly and berries and mistletoe, the scent of pine trees and beauty of the snow, the sound of bells, the glitter of the city, and carols drifting through the quiet night. But most important was the deeper meaning, the essence of Christmas—love. Each scene tumbled through Julie's mind—her family, the schoolroom, Eddy and Billy Kingston, cookies and caroling, Mexico and a white Bible and Allen, dear Allen....

Julie closed her eyelids, and a contented smile crossed her face.

God had given her Christmas, every Christmas she had known. He had left each lovely memory to be remembered, to be treasured. He had intended that she remember the love that was given each Christmas, from the very first Christmas when He gave the supreme Gift, right on through each of Julie's Christmases and every beautiful memory of love. She knew, now, that she must grow up and learn to return this love. Suddenly she felt a warm surge of appreciation of the expressions of love *she* had received—from Momma, the relatives, Miss Blossom, Eddy, Billy, Norma Kingston, Mrs. Donaldson, the kids at church, Casey Dunlap and the chorus, Sandra, Mrs. Macintosh, even Allen, but especially God.

In the coming years, would she not remember this year and the love and other good things it had brought? Somehow, in remembering the Riverdale Youth Club's banquet, she would forget that Allen took Riti. She would lose the vision of rival Sylvia Hawkins when she recalled how she always ate lunch with her pal Marshall James while the muffled strains of "White Christmas" and "Winter Wonderland" floated through the noisy school cafeteria.

Now, as suddenly as it had come, the storm ceased. And the sun, shining through the moist air, created a rainbow. Julie saw it first over in the apricot orchard—her Christmas rainbow, symbol of love....

The next morning, the two girls walked down the street on their way to the banquet hall. "Oh, Julie, I'm so excited!" cried Sandra. "I guess it's just the atmosphere, so near to Christmas and all. It's the banquet tonight and Christmas Eve on Sunday with LeRoy...." Her voice trailed off.

"Yes," Julie agreed, smiling, "Christmastime is a *very* gay season."

"Well," said Sandra, "I'm glad you're a little more optimistic this morning. Ah, Julie, how are you going to spend Christmas this year?" There was an expectant teasing twinkle in Sandra's voice.

"Oh, I don't know," Julie shrugged. "Probably have dinner with Momma and Grandpa Philip and cousin Sue and Uncle Jake and all the rest of the relatives. We'll probably go for a ride in the country Christmas afternoon. I don't know," Julie shrugged again. "It really doesn't matter as long as everybody has love—the Christmas spirit—down deep in their hearts."

Sandra cocked her head and raised her eyebrows. "Very good, Julie. But what about Allen?"

"Oh, I guess he'll have a nice Christmas, too," Julie answered with a twinkle. At once she grew very serious. "Sandra, I don't need to tell you how much in love I have been with Allen. He was everything a girl could want—and more. But—" She bit her lip and shook her head. She was silent only a moment, and then she tossed her dark curls back and shrugged lightly. "But love is something very mysterious. Sometimes it's so real, but so intangible. It's like Christmas. For some, it comes for but a brief, beautiful moment, then—then it's gone. But it's gone only because people can't or won't hold on to it."

"Allen couldn't hold on to it, but you're holding it—for Allen?" Sandra ventured.

"No," Julie replied, surprising Sandra. "No," she repeated, slowly and deliberately, "I'm not in love with Allen Macintosh."

The words stunned Sandra! "Wha—wh-why?"

"Love responds only to love, Sandra, and not to hate. Allen hurt me, but it's all over now. Christmas means more than sentimentality."

Suddenly Julie stopped. There, above Sandra's meadow, beyond the misty hills, Julie saw it again—her symbol of Christmas love. Sandra hadn't seen it yet, and she looked at Julie in silent wonder.

"Sandra," she said with a quiet smile, "I caught it yesterday—that rainbow you told me to stop chasing. It encircled the moon last night and has left a beautiful glow in my heart."

"Julie," Sandra giggled, "are you all right?"

Julie chuckled, but she smiled in serious happiness. "It's just that I've found the true meaning of Christmas—love. Allen's love was one kind of love, but it's not the only kind. I've been so blind and selfish, not letting myself be happy just because Allen doesn't 'love' me this Christmas. We can express love in so many ways, as the past years have proven. But this year I'm giving love to my own dear family. Maybe next year—and the years after that—love *will* be with Allen again, I don't know. Maybe not." Julie's eyes still fastened on the rainbow. "Maybe someday, somewhere—at an exotic dinner, by an ancient cathedral, or on a college campus—I'll find the man of my dreams. He'll be all of Allen—and more. He'll bring love and laughter and music into my life. Maybe" —she smiled slightly— "he'll even be an only child like me." She stood still and looked at her friend. "Sandra, maybe it'll happen at Christmastime, and that rainbow will be in the sky."

"Julie," Sandra said, looking at her in amazement, "you *have* caught a rainbow—the rainbow of Christmas love."

"But even until that magic day, whenever it happens, love will fill every Christmas. That's what Christmas is all about!"

EPILOGUE: JULIE SCOTT Davidson

Julie couldn't see ahead to the *next* Christmas when she *would* be with Allen again, sharing a deeper kind of love; or to *two* Christmases ahead and the exciting romantic whirl with Mike Kirwin who would treat her like an exotic princess; or to *four* Christmases ahead when she would reach a maturity she couldn't imagine now and find herself engaged to Howard Davidson and busily planning a wedding for a whole ten months away; or of *the* Christmas, her first Christmas as Howard's wife in their cozy apartment, and the true love that she and Howard and God would share.... Julie couldn't know all these details, but she knew the rainbow would still be in the sky every Christmas.

I know, for I am Julie. And each Christmas brings a wealth of love I have never known before. It is Christmas again, my second Christmas with Howard; and it is more wonderful than the first. And, yes, Howard is an only child like me.

Sandra and Bob, her husband, are sharing Christmas.

Allen is spending this Christmas with his bride, Shirley.

The carolers still sing. And everywhere there are Mrs. Donaldsons and Norma Kingstons and Miss Blossoms and Mommas and high school choruses—even Billys and Eddys and Caseys and Allens and Mikes—who are expressing their love, too, in their own special way.

And my Christmas rainbow *is* still in the sky.

"And This Is Forever"

Written late in Julie's junior year at Highview Academy, this story is based on Highview characters rather than Riverdale characters. Strangely, the main characters are not even among Julie's actual best friends at Highview but are among the most popular and prominent Highview students. Julie picks up on what she sees as an interesting storyline to write about.

PART 1. BONNIE AND Jim

The night was cool and crisp and bright, and the crescent moon glimmered on the grassy meadow. Hand in hand, a boy and girl strolled across the carpet of green. The June breeze blew softly through her satiny hair and wafted the refreshing scent of peach blossoms. He reached for a small bough of the delicate flowers and broke it off for her as she smiled affectionately.

"For you, my pretty one," he said.

"Jim," she said, her soft voice carrying an almost serious tone, "did you ever wonder how two people can be so happy?"

Slightly surprised—for Bonnie seldom was so bold in philosophizing—he squeezed her hand tightly. "And why is everything so good and beautiful to those same two?"

"Because," she said simply, "God made it that way."

"And," he added, "God is love."

Bonnie was silent, not knowing quite how to interpret his words. *Was he really in love with her? Was that why he said that?*

Now they came to the road that led back to Bonnie's house. "When we get back," he said, his voice pleasant but business-like, "let's practice some more for tomorrow."

Tomorrow! That was the Talent Festival—how could she forget? For weeks Jim had been practicing for this big day. Tomorrow would decide his future....

Her mind went back to many years ago; in fact, almost as long as she could remember, she had known Jim. There had been the Saturday night motion pictures at the college, and the eighth-grade banquet, their first actual date. Then there were the bike rides and the picnics in the park, and the many, many times he had come over to practice. Through the years their musical skills, and their friendship, had grown together.

The clock was striking ten as Bonnie's slim fingers trickled over the piano keyboard and the last notes from Jim's clarinet faded into silence. "Very good!" She applauded and grinned.

"You're the one they should clap for," he said. "I couldn't do it without you." He put the instrument in its case.

When she rose from the piano stool, she felt his hand touch her waist lightly.

"You're a good girl," he whispered.

Just then there was the sound of a hotrod motor and brakes screeching into the driveway.

"Oh," she said, "Johnny must be home."

"*Your* twin?" he teased. "*This* early on a Saturday night?"

They laughed, and then Jim opened the door. "I'll be by about two o'clock tomorrow," he said, "okay?"

She nodded. "Goodnight, Jim."

Minutes later, Bonnie heard the back door slam and her brother's footsteps in the kitchen. She entered the kitchen and found him raiding the refrigerator.

"Oh, hi, Sis." He looked up sheepishly as he brought out a couple of two-day-old doughnuts.

"Well, hello, Romeo," she said, sitting down. "Who did you take out?"

He pulled out a chair across from her and took a big bite from a doughnut. "Renée," he said coolly.

"Johnny!" Bonnie gasped.

He grinned. "What's the matter?"

She giggled. "You little stinker!"

"She's quite a girl," he said, dreamily staring past his sister.

"But what's happened to Ken?" she asked, ignoring Johnny's mood.

"Oh, I think he's going back with Cheri," was his answer.

"Well, it's about time. I hope it lasts this time. But I don't know," she said thoughtfully. "It's happened so many times." *It's happened so many times.* Yes, she remembered when Renée once had Bonnie's own Jim. It was only last year when Bonnie and Jim had drifted apart. That was a strange world, that world without Jim. She remembered the unfeelingness and emotion, the independence yet mixed-upness of it all. Even now she halfway smiled as she saw herself slam a locker in a moment of fierce emotion—so unlike her gentle nature—and the times he had come over to practice while he was still going with Renée. Bonnie had been so cold—so different from the usually friendly Bonnie Mayfield. Even after Renée and Jim broke up and Jim wanted to date Bonnie again—although a few parents forbade it—her hurt pride made her act like she really didn't want to go out with him, anyway. He had tried to convince her she was his best girl, but then when he walked to school with Renée the very next day—that did it!

"*Are* you, Bonnie?" Johnny's voice interrupted her reminiscing, and his voice carried a tone of urgency as if he had asked her before.

"Oh," —she came back to reality— "am I what?"

"Playing for Jim tomorrow?" he finished.

She nodded as she rose from her chair, yawning. "'Night, Johnny," she said, wandering toward her room.

PART 2. THE SEMI-FINALISTS

Morning dawned cool and cheerful. Bonnie stretched and opened her pretty blue eyes. Six fifteen, the clock said. She yawned, turned over, and the next thing she knew the warm sunbeams were shining into her face and someone was rapping loudly on her bedroom door.

"Who is it?" Bonnie called in a raspy, half-asleep voice.

"It's just me, Bonnie," returned a feminine voice.

"Oh, come on in, Carol," she said, getting out of bed.

A vivacious curly-headed contemporary walked in and flopped on a chair. "My, but you're up bright and early this morning. And *so* wide awake!"

Bonnie smiled and rubbed her eyes. "What time is it?"

"Almost 10:30," Carol answered. "Are you going to play for Jim this afternoon?"

"Yes!" Bonnie started. "And I've got to get the house cleaned and my homework done before two o'clock!" With that, she got dressed hurriedly while Carol talked on.

"I just wondered if I could borrow your little pink purse for tonight," she said. "Nick called and asked me out tonight!"

"How neat!" Bonnie was really glad for her friend—she had tried so hard to be the girl that he wanted. "Sure."

"We're going double with Ken and Cheri—they're back together now! The guys are taking us out to eat, then we'll come by the high school later to see who wins the Talent Festival." Carol went on and on excitedly, and then suddenly she stopped. "You're lucky, Bonnie."

Bonnie stopped brushing her hair. "Me?" she chuckled. She could see her reflection in the mirror and the things behind her in the room. She was an ordinary plain-looking girl, living in an average house. "Goodness, why?" she asked.

Carol shrugged. "Well, Jim. You can be so sure of him." Bonnie knew that neither Carol nor Cheri was sure of Nick or Ken. "But even if you didn't have Jim," Carol went on, "I don't think it would change your cheerful personality." And it was true. Bonnie's sparkling eyes and contagious smile on her long freckled face, her willingness to work, the interest she took in anybody she talked to—this made her very attractive to all who knew her.

"Well, don't try *too* hard," Bonnie said, seeming to sense that Carol had been comparing herself and Nick with Bonnie and Jim. "I didn't pay *any* attention to Jim, even after he quit Renée."

"That's what puzzles me," Carol said, shaking her head as she got up. "Well, I've got to be going. I promised Cheri I'd be over for lunch."

Bonnie fetched the little pink purse. Then Carol was gone.

The time passed quickly. The house was sparkling clean; and Bonnie, in a fresh cotton print, was just closing her American government textbook when the doorbell rang.

"Have time to go over it once?" Jim asked, stepping inside.

"Sure!" She smiled sweetly. "Aren't you scared?"

"Tell you a secret," he said. "I'm petrified!"

When they finished, Jim escorted her out to his car. It all seemed too familiar. Renée might have sat in the center next to Jim, but Bonnie didn't. Ever since their first date after the Renée episode, Jim and Bonnie had been as good friends as ever, but nothing more. It was only recently that he had even hinted that she was someone special—that is, except for the time when she had asked him, "But why aren't you taking Renée to the A.S.B. social?"

And he had answered simply, "Because I like you better."

Talented, handsome, athletic Jim Barker was a silent, almost mysterious easy-going gentleman—that was the way she liked him. There was only one short year before they'd be going to college, but of course quite a few years before marriage— Marriage! How could she dare think of it! She glanced at Jim whose serene steady eyes were intent on the road and on his driving. He smiled warmly, but if he had sensed any of Bonnie's thoughts he didn't let on.

The people were already filling the assembly hall when Jim and Bonnie arrived. He tuned up his instrument. Then they went backstage to wait for their turn on the program. Many others performed their numbers, classic and comedy, fast and slow, light and dramatic, mostly amateur, but some were superb. Among them was Jim's beautiful and difficult, "Fantasia in D Minor."

Finally, at a quarter to five, the emcee spoke. "Our result from the applause meter shows which five of the young people you have chosen as the best. Will you semi-finalists please come back as I call your names? Jim Barker!..." The audience broke into applause, and Bonnie gave a little squeal of delight. She was too happy to care who the other four were. She only heard the emcee conclude, "And we'll see you again at eight o'clock tonight when the final winners are chosen."

"Oh, Jim, I'm so proud of you!" she said when she had found him.

He squeezed her hand affectionately for a moment as he said, "You were half of it, angel." Then, in a completely different mood, he said, "Say, how would you like to have dinner at The Blue Rose?"

The fanciest restaurant in town? "I'd love to!" she said.

PART 3. THE BLUE ROSE Dining Room

Candlelight and soft music filled The Blue Rose Dining Room as a tuxedoed server showed Jim and Bonnie to a table for two. The setting was perfect; now it was up to Jim....

Several tables away, Bonnie saw Ken and Cheri with Nick and Carol. Across the crowded room, Carol gave Bonnie a knowing look as Bonnie remembered Carol's words, "You can be so sure of him." Now Bonnie thought, *If only you knew, Carol, just how uncertain I really am just now.*

"What would you like, Bonnie?" It was Jim's voice that broke into her thoughts.

"Oh." She looked up, half-startled, first at Jim and then at the server who stood ready to take their order.

When the food was served to them, Jim bowed his head and asked a blessing on the food before they ate. That was another thing about Jim—he was a Christian, the best kind, and not ashamed of it. As far as Bonnie was concerned, that made everything complete.

The conversation naturally drifted to the Talent Festival, to what had happened and what might happen. For the past six years Jim had taken part in the Festival, but this was the first time he had made it to the chosen five. Until now he had been relatively calm; now his intense excitement showed through.

"Oh, Bonnie!" he breathed. "Would it be possible that I, James Gordon Barker, could win a cup tonight?"

"Of course, it is," she answered sweetly. "If anybody could, you can, Jim."

He sighed. "Oh, if only!"

"By the way," she asked, "what's in the crystal cup this year?"

"It's a neat prize," he answered. "A full year's music lessons on any instrument from any teacher anywhere in the United States, Canada, *and* Europe!"

"Oh, boy!" exclaimed Bonnie. "That's not a bad deal! And you'll have just one year with Professor Waldo before college, too."

"Well," Jim hesitated, "I'm not so sure."

"What do you mean," asked Bonnie, sensing the seriousness in his voice, "that you're not so sure?"

"Bonnie," he began, "I didn't want to tell you this before—I'll be in Austria next year."

"Austria!" Her fork stopped in mid-air. "*Next* year?"

"You see," he explained, "Professor Waldo thinks I'm good enough to go to the Bogenhaden Academy—it's a sort of junior college—and by about Christmas of next year I should be ready for the Music Conservatory at the University of Vienna—so he says."

"But that means you won't be able to graduate with our class, then."

"I know," he said. "I'll just get my diploma, and then it's back to the books. But it'll be good to get to study music there—the atmosphere and everything, you know—with the best teachers and good facilities, then maybe weekend trips to Venice or Rome...." A faint smile played on his face, and there was a far-away look in his cool gray eyes.

Bonnie was strangely silent. This sudden news was quite surprising and somewhat disappointing, although down deep she really wanted things to work out for Jim's best good. But she must not let Jim see her hurt. "What's first prize, in the gold cup?" she asked.

"Oh." He came back to earth. "That one's *really* fabulous. They're giving away a scholarship to one of the big music colleges—University of Vienna included—plus the year's music lessons *plus* your choice of either a brand-new instrument (piano excluded) or the price equivalent in sheet music."

"Wow!" exclaimed Bonnie. "Who's paying for all this?"

"Some music association," he shrugged. "The silver cup is a choice between the music lessons and the scholarship."

"But even that would be a nice thing to take to Austria with you," she said, trying to not change the subject anymore.

"But dreams like that wouldn't come true in real life—in *my* life."

"Sure they could, Jim." Bonnie's interest was genuine. She was going to lose him, anyway. "I have faith in you. You're a semi-finalist, aren't you?"

"Yes, but look at my competition. That Mary Lind and her violin, Ted Jones on the piano—you heard them play—they're good!"

"You're good, too," she spoke in mild rebuke. "Besides, even if you don't win a cup, you've got that fine education in Austria waiting for you."

"Maybe." His excitement had almost turned into discouragement.

"Maybe?" Bonnie's curiosity and sympathy were aroused at once.

"You'll keep this confidential, won't you, Bonnie?" Jim's voice was low. His head dropped slightly, and he raised his eyes to look at her. "It's just the financial part."

"What?" Bonnie spoke with incredulity. "Dr. Barker's son?!"

"Yeah, Dad's not so over-enthused about me leaving home so soon. Says if I go, I have to pay my own way, every penny. You know he wanted me to get a job in his clinic next summer, then work part time and go to New City College. Mom's all for me going, but you know how high-class the University of Vienna is—best school in all of Europe, almost. Professor Waldo said he'll do everything he can to see me put at Bogenhaden, but I'll still have it pretty rough for a while—if I don't get that scholarship. There's a chance," he added, "that I might not even go."

A feeling of half-hope and half-sympathy arose spontaneously in Bonnie. She looked lovingly at him, a strong husky youth but with a chivalrous tenderness.... Suddenly, as she realized the growing silence, she wanted to speak, but somehow—as it rarely happened—she couldn't seem to find the right words. Finally, she said, "I wish the very best for you, Jim, always." And she meant it.

When Jim paid the check, he and Bonnie made their way back to the school. The audience filled the hall, and dramatic floodlights shone down onto the stage. Once again, backstage, they waited with the other semi-finalists. Jim's hands were sweaty at first—Bonnie was holding one—but after the program got started, a foreign, almost weird expression came over Jim's face. There was a strange calmness in his eyes, and his hands were dry and completely relaxed.

PART 4. THE WINNERS Announced

When Bonnie preceded Jim onto the stage and sat down at the piano, there was a brief, tense moment before the clear, cool notes of Jim's clarinet once again drifted through the silent hall. It was just like they had always practiced it—first the plaintive melody-theme, then here and there a fast difficult run that faded into a harmonic work of art and swelled into the full rich overtures, then once again a lone soft voice, a colorful variation, a frilly bit, and majestic tones until the listener was in a different world. Then once again the audience swelled the applause.

Backstage once more, Jim sighed silently; but Bonnie sensed his deep relief. He put his clarinet away when she touched his arm. "Don't do that," she said. "When they take your picture with the cup, you'll want to have your clarinet with you." She giggled a little as she spoke, and he just had to smile.

"You funny girl," he said, putting his finger lightly to her chin. "I won't win."

Jim and Bonnie, with the others who had already performed, went to sit in the audience. While the judges were deliberating, the community comedian and the Music Club's skit made up an interesting program. But to the five—and the ones close to them—it seemed like an eternity before they decided.

At long last, the emcee once again stood on the stage. His voice rang, cutting through the silent hush that settled on the entire crowd. "As you know, the time has come to announce our three finalists. The two remaining will automatically receive the consolation prize—the $50 check which we will send to them.

"Now the winner of the crystal cup—the music lessons—a deserving young musician, Julie Scott!"

There was applause as the young accordionist walked on stage to accept her prize. But Bonnie and Jim exchanged puzzled glances as if to say, "Was Julie *that* good?"

"Well," Jim whispered to Bonnie, "Ted Jones and Mary Lind are sure to get the other cups."

But Bonnie said nothing.

"The silver cup," the emcee continued, "belongs to a very skilled young lady—performer of Beethoven's *Intermezzo*—Mary Jo Lind!"

Again, there was applause, and Mary Lind walked on stage. "As you know, Mary Jo, you have your choice between a year's music lessons and a $500 scholarship."

With every word the emcee spoke, Bonnie grew more and more tense. For those fleeting moments, she didn't care that Jim was going away to get his education, even though it meant losing him. Jim *had* to win. But now the doubts were growing in *her* mind, too. Ted Jones *was* pretty good....

"And the winner of this year's grand prize—the scholarship, the music lessons, and sheet music—is a young man whom I think we all will agree is worthy of the gold cup, a young man who is rightly a credit to our community, and whom I'm sure we can with great pride esteem this honor. Congratulations to—" The emcee paused drastically, and Jim had almost whispered, "Good for Ted!" when he heard— "Jim Barker!"

Something like a bolt of lightning struck him as he just sat, stunned, his clarinet still clutched tightly in his hand. Bonnie almost had to push him toward the stage. Then she sat, beaming, as she watched him—her Jim—standing in the spotlight. The applause was loud and long. Cameras flashed as the mayor and the principal shook hands with Jim.

The program was over, and reporters flocked around Jim. Other well-meaning congratulators swarmed about him.

When the crowd thinned out, someone called Bonnie to the front "for a picture of the hero's piano-player." But before she had time to speak to Jim, some big shot took him away to interview him or something. Even to this day, Bonnie cannot quite explain the feeling inside. Her pride in him was mingled with a bit of sarcasm and even loneliness. Mixed all together was the ego, the left-out feeling, the love, the bitterness, the sympathy, the frustration, the hopeless hope—it was all there. Like a run-down clock, the time passed until Bonnie realized, dazedly, that she stood alone just outside the door of the empty hall. Seeing Jim nowhere, she started for his car to wait for him there.

PART 5. JIM'S PROPOSAL

Soon Jim came and, without a word, opened the door for her then got in on the other side and started the car. For the first time in all her life, she felt ill at ease with him.

Finally, she said, with a trace of enthusiasm, "Congratulations, Jim."

He looked at her and smiled in recognition. "Sorry I took so long to get out, but—man!—the publicity you get. I just couldn't get away."

Bonnie smiled and carried on the conversation, but somehow it didn't seem the same.

Presently Jim stopped the car, got out, walked around and opened Bonnie's door. He took her hand and whispered, "Want to go for a walk?"

If it surprised her, she didn't show it. She got out and looked around. They were in the country, the same meadow where just 24 hours ago, they had walked hand in hand. But it seemed so long ago now, so far, far in the distant past. The moon was fuller tonight, silvering the green growing things and creating a half-mysterious, half-romantic atmosphere. The breeze barely stirred, and the delicate scent of the peach blossoms was faint. Their conversation had ceased; and Bonnie, in the thick stillness, wanted to fall into Jim's arms and cry and cry. But she knew she mustn't let a teardrop escape her eyelids.

Jim spoke now and Bonnie listened, not knowing exactly how she should feel about everything. "They've made plane reservations for me for some time the last of next week, so I guess this time next week I'll be in Salzburg. Professor Waldo wants me to take two summer courses."

Jim would be gone in just *one week?* She realized it, but it was not as hard as she might have expected it to be. She only looked up into his eyes, and Jim smiled.

He continued talking about the courses he would take, what it would be like to study in a foreign country, the kind of teachers he might have, the books he would use, where he might work, and everything that had to do with his newly acquired future. And while he talked, so earnestly and happily, Bonnie's mixed-up feelings turned into a mutual sharing of his happiness and a mature outlook on life—her life and Jim's life—a courageous acceptance of losing him to Austria, and a genuine pride that her Jim was a master of tomorrow's musical world.

Now they stood on a little knoll overlooking the meadow. To the left was the peach orchard, and to the right a little patch of woods. In the silence, they could hear the gurgling sound of a hidden brook. Jim dropped Bonnie's hand and pointed straight ahead. In the same soft expressional tone, he said, "Do you see that uncleared land, that spot of ground 'way over there?"

Bonnie looked.

"Someday," he went on, slipping his arm around her, "that land will be plowed and cultivated. And nestled between the field and the orchard will be a rustic cottage with a white picket fence and red roses. And it will be waiting for two lucky people on their way home from Vienna."

At this, Bonnie looked up at him.

He smiled in admiration at the innocent smile on her pretty face. His eyes showed a devoted affection just as hopeful as his dreams and as deep as the dedication to his music.

"Five years," he continued, "isn't so long when two are in love. We'll date others, if you want, but I'm coming back to you, the wonderful girl who has made and will always make a wonderful life possible."

"Me?" Bonnie chuckled a bit. "Make a wonderful life possible?"

He smiled, but his voice was still serious. "Your patience in practicing so much with me and helping me to win a start toward the life I want. Besides, all the encouragement and inspiration you have brought through the years I have known you—no other girl has kept me so close to God. Another thing" —and he chuckled a bit— "I thought maybe you would be a little resentful because of all your hard work in getting me ready to win the gold cup then having everything fly away to Austria—but you just aren't like that."

She blushed slightly and drew in a deep breath. How near she had been to being the very opposite, and how glad she was that she had said nothing!

She felt his hand on her shoulder as he drew her closer. "Bonnie, sweetheart, I love you," he said simply. "Five years—we can do it—will you marry me then? Do you love me enough to?"

Her voice was choked with the unspilled tears of joy. "Yes, Jim," she said calmly and sweetly. "I do."

"Darling!" he whispered as his lips touched hers to seal the spoken vow. Bonnie could see in his eyes the fame, then the grassy valley—the heaven on earth for them. To him, her voice was the sound of music, the sound of a raptured theme, of church bells....

He spoke again. "And this is forever."

Anne's Christmas Valentine

The timeframe of this story is two years after the Christmas in "November Rain" when Julie and Allen first fell in love. Now it's best friend Sandra Anne Lee's turn to find her forever-after love, Bob Miller. Sandra goes to La Paloma College for her freshman year but comes home for Christmas 1962. Unfortunately, it's also a time of great sadness when Sandra Lee's mother dies. How can she deal with the ecstasy of Bob's marriage proposal when she has just had to say goodbye to her loving mother?!

PART 1. CHRISTMAS EVE

The December night's sky was clear, and the diamond-like stars twinkled with holiday brilliance as a dozen and a half youthful voices rang through the cold air with the clear sweet melodies of Christmas carols. Sandra Anne Lee strolled along with the others, half-wishing Bob could only be here tonight. She looked in admiration at her best friends, Julie and Allen, who walked ahead hand in hand. In just a day or two, Bob *would* be here. Then the four of them would spend Christmas together.

"Hey, Sandra, have a cookie!" She looked up to see that the carolers had stopped in front of a house where a little old warm-hearted lady had given cookies to the young singers. And there stood Peter Macintosh, Allen's little brother, with cookies in an outstretched hand. Sandra smiled warmly as she thanked him.

The pleasant evening passed all too quickly, even for half-lonely Sandra. Despite Bob's lengthy absence, Sandra was happy; she was in love. But once back at the church, Mrs. Betty Macintosh, the pastor's wife, greeted Sandra solemnly. "The hospital just phoned," she said.

A surge of fear shot through Sandra's body. Her mother! But it couldn't be—it just couldn't be. She remembered last July when her mother had had the first terrible attack, and then the operation. It had been a dreadful, unreal nightmare. She felt Bob's hand clutching her own as they prayed during those crucial hours. And then there was the miraculous pull-through and road to recovery. Then it happened all over again. Now for months her mother had lain in bed, sometimes seeming to be better, sometimes not. But Sandra had long ago accepted the cruel reality and adjusted her life to it. Yet now she felt very weak, as she looked straight into Mrs. Macintosh's deep blue eyes.

"The doctor says only a few more hours at the most," she continued. "Your father is there now; do you want me to take you? Or if you want to go to the young people's social, I'll take you. Whatever you say."

A brief smile broke on Sandra's face. Mrs. Macintosh was *so* sweet. Besides, Sandra wasn't the dismal type. She decided quickly. She would go to the hospital and then go to the social.

Mr. Lee, who was staying with his wife at the hospital that night, was very sad. Sandra's eyes were not dry as she left her mother's room. She knew it might be the last time she would ever see her this side of heaven.

Of course, vivacious Sandra could not fully enjoy the social, but she decided *not* to be gloomy. They would reunite some sweet day, Daddy and her and Mommie. Jesus had promised it, and now she clung desperately to what Bob had often brought to her attention, quoting Romans 8:28, "All things work together for good..."

It wasn't until Sunday when Sandra was at Julie's house that she broke down in front of her. Mrs. Lee had pulled through the night; but the tension seemed to be even greater. Half-relieved, half-anticipating she-didn't-know-what, Sandra blurted out in a tone that almost surprised Julie, "Why does Bob have to be coming here now anyway?!" Then she went through all his faults while almost in the same breath reviewing his virtues.

Julie listened patiently to it all, trying to understand her best friend. She knew how much Sandra really wanted to be with Bob. She had even stayed last night, upon Mrs. Macintosh's invitation, at Macintoshes' house, since that's where Bob would go first. Yet she secretly longed to be all alone for a while.

Then Sandra talked about college, about next year up north at Pacific Christian College with Bob, about the years after that when Julie and Allen would be there, and the years after that when the four of them would be in evangelism. Dreams, yes, but it helped to release Sandra's pent-up emotions. That night she slept until nearly ten the next morning, December 24.

The shrill sound of the telephone awakened Sandra. She heard Mrs. Macintosh answer the phone and then call her. "Sandra, this call is for you."

"All right, Julie," she groaned, crawling out of bed. But when she answered the phone, her heart pounded hard.

"Bob? Bob!" she cried. "Oh, I can hardly believe it! How long are you staying in Riverdale? Have you seen your 'little sis' Julie yet?" And so it went.

Sandra spent the afternoon at Macintoshes' house. For four long months, 600 miles had separated them; now nothing, not even Pastor Don Macintosh's presence, stopped Sandra and Bob from falling into each other's arms.

They spent the afternoon at Macintoshes' busily preparing for a Christmas Eve supper. Mr. Lee, whom the pastor and his wife called Harry, and Sandra's Aunt Jane would be there, too. And of course, Julie would be there if Allen had anything to say about it!

It was a good old-fashioned Christmas Eve—everything from a prettily decorated tree to Allen's youngest brother Kenny spilling milk on the living room rug. The supper, eaten by candlelight, was simple yet delightful. After supper Harry and Jane and Betty and Don, as they called each other, chatted. Peter and Kenny watched as four of the happiest young people in the world talked and laughed, sometimes reminiscing. They passed around their placemats for each other to sign, then let a drop of red wax from the burning candles fall onto each placemat.

Sandra seemed to be at the zenith of happiness. Even now, her mind wandered back to over eight months ago when it had all started. Then it was the grade school teacher, Raymond Pierce, whom she had met at the St. Patrick's Day party. Soon afterwards, Raymond had introduced Sandra to his best friend Bob Miller and his then-girlfriend Wanda, with whom they double dated frequently. After that, Bob and Julie had dated. And what could be better than best friends together? Then there was the marriage proposal from Raymond—a sudden, exciting thing that nearly swept Sandra off her feet! Sandra's graduation came, and Raymond didn't want to wait. But Sandra wasn't ready. Summer came, and with it came Sandra's decision. Sandra was firm in saying no, and soon Raymond reluctantly told her goodbye and headed back to his hometown to teach school.

Depressed and out of a job, Bob had temporarily stayed in his trailer on Julie Scott's family's place. Then in July, Julie and her family took a vacation back East and Bob stayed at their house to take care of their yard and pets. That was when Sandra and Bob had fallen in love. Julie had gone on vacation and Allen started writing letters to her using blue stationery. Fortunately (for Bob), Allen and Julie got back together, so Bob and Sandra were free to get together.

All this ran through Sandra's mind in just a moment as she breathed a secret sigh—now Bob was hers, all hers....

PART 2. THE PROPOSAL

The glittering gifts around the tree, the smell of pine and holly and persimmon cookies, the Christmas records on the hi-fi, and the pitter-patter of gentle rain all added to the cozy togetherness as Bob and Sandra and Julie and Allen basked in the warmth of the cheery fireplace. Kenny had gone to bed and Peter was reading to him, and the grownups were in the kitchen making popcorn. Snuggled up close to Bob, Sandra could see Allen and Julie, lively but serious, young and foolish and sentimental, yet sincerely Christian. But now Sandra gave her full attention to Bob.

"I love you *so* much, babe doll," he was whispering, not loud enough for anyone else, except for Allen and Julie—if they had been listening—to hear. "Princess," he murmured, "won't it be wonderful when we get married! Just like Don and Betty..." He went on, but the words "when we get married" rang through Sandra's mind. To be a minister's wife—that was her dream! Bob was a junior in college now; only three short years more. And it could be less, since the denomination needed young ministers so much. He would make a good pastor, one of the best, there was no doubt about it. Sandra recalled those summer nights she had spent with Bob in her family's garage, studying the Bible and prophecy. He had explained everything so clearly, yet with tact and love.

But to be a "Mrs." so soon, or even engaged! Even now Bob was saying, "It's Christmas, honey, and remember our promise." Sandra remembered. On the day Bob left for college they had agreed that if they still felt the same way about each other, and especially if they had dated others—which they both had done—well, what was left but engagement?

Now Sandra and Bob sat in silence, but she could feel his searching eyes wanting to look deep into her heart. He loved her—she knew that—but why must she answer now? If Daddy ever knew, he would kill her!

"Tomorrow, Princess," Bob whispered in a way that almost melted her—but not quite. Then Bob called to Allen, "Hey, fellow, it's getting late. I guess we'd better take our girls home soon."

And so, after the boys each placed his gift, with instructions to not open until Christmas morning, into the respective hands of the delighted girls, they escorted them home in the usual manner. But Sandra could not quickly fall asleep.

Surely God meant for them to be together. No one else in either his or her life had supplied such a feeling of completeness. No other boy had made Christ seem so real and personal to her, had given her incentive to study her often dust-covered Bible, and had generated the deepening desire to be a minister's—an evangelist's—wife. No other girl had been quite like Sandra to Bob, had inspired him to go back to college, or had been such a cheerful, sympathetic, and loving source of inspiration. Yes, miracles had happened and were happening.

The thought of marrying Bob was wonderful, but that would be a long time away. But being engaged! And tomorrow! She knew Bob would not force an answer, but the anxiousness in his eyes, the half-hidden hurt in his voice would be even worse....

Christmas morning dawned, typically southern Californian, clear and sunny. But even with Sandra's sunny spirit, Christmas could not be quite the same at the Lee household. With Dorothy Lee in a coma, the silent walls and the strange emptiness of the lonely house were almost unbearable. Yet, they had put the cheery Christmas tree up as usual by the window in the living room. Now Sandra and Harry would spend Christmas day at Macintoshes.

With the kindness of Pastor Macintosh, Mr. Lee had accepted calmly the saddening experience concerning the one he loved so dearly. She had been a wonderful wife and mother. Eighteen-year-old Sandra was the living proof of that. Harry, like Sandra, now had the calm assurance of being reunited—someday....

Julie's cousin Sue came to spend the rest of the vacation week, so Sue and Julie, Allen, Peter, Sandra, and Bob spent most of the afternoon at Macintoshes' playing with Peter's new game, helping with Christmas dinner, listening to Bob play his guitar, or just talking around the fireplace. They had exchanged presents in love—a homemade shirt, a vest, stuffed animals, lovely black gloves and purse.

Later that evening Sandra found herself in an overstuffed chair with Bob on his knees by the chair and Sandra's hand in his own—a pretty eighteenth-century picture of a perfect proposal!

"Sandra," he said, "we've known each other quite a while now. And don't you think it's about time—"

"Time?" she said with a mischievous sparkle. "Oh, I believe the time is 9:43."

"Well, uh, what I mean is, uh…"

"Oh, I agree, definitely."

"Uh, look, honey, we love each other…don't we?"

Sandra's mock seriousness changed to the old familiar smile as she nodded, then quickly changed back again with a nonchalant, "Of course."

"Well, what I'm trying to say is…"

"Oh, are you trying to *say* something?"

"Sandra,"—dramatic silence— "will you marry me?"

Sandra, trying harder than ever to keep a straight face, held out a dangling hand on a stiffened outstretched arm. "Kiss me."

With graceful elegance, he pressed his lips against her hand. "Sandra Anne Lee, my dear"—with more and more drama— "*will* you?"

She looked blankly at him for a moment and then at her audience. "Well, folks, stay tuned again next year, same time, same station."

The other kids could hold back the laughter no longer. It was all so ridiculously funny. To everyone, including Bob and Sandra, it was a great show. But down deep inside, Sandra knew that Bob really meant what he said, every syllable.

PART 3. THE VALENTINE

Before they said the goodbyes that night, somehow Bob and Sandra found a moment to be alone. "This is for you," he whispered, as he pressed something into her hand and lightly kissed her forehead.

Puzzled, she looked into her hand to find a small plain white plastic box. Opening it, she found a small fuzzy honeybee mounted on a tiny wire stand and a pale purple orchid on a greeting tag with these simple words, reminding her of a sweet old-fashioned valentine: "To my Sandra, Will you 'bee' mine? I love you much. Bob."

She looked into his warm blue eyes, filled with sacred love, and this time she really melted. That simple gift meant more to Sandra than any fancy gloves or purse, even if they made them of gold. How could she resist saying "yes"?

The week passed all too quickly for Peter and Allen and Julie and Sue, but especially for Bob and Sandra. Then it happened.

It was when Harry and Sandra were in church that Dorothy Lee slipped away. But they were prepared, emotionally and spiritually. And being in church was the next best place to being by her side that Mr. Lee felt he could have been.

The kids—Bob, Sandra, Peter, Allen, Julie, Sue, and two others, Sam and Alice—had planned a drive to the mountains. Sandra, of course, stayed with her father. But she would not let the others cancel their trip to the snow. That was just Sandra.

Because of the circumstances, Bob did not see his beloved one until Sunday, just a few hours before he had to head back north to Pacific Christian College. His bus would leave at 7:00 p.m. from Perris, which was sixteen miles from Riverdale. Allen would drive him to the station, and of course the girls were going along.

What a mad rush! One always dislikes leaving good friends, especially ones like Macintoshes. And as hard as Bob and Allen tried, they weren't ready to pick up the girls until after 6:30. And they still had to get gas!

When Allen went to the door for Julie, he whispered quickly and excitedly, "Guess what! Sandra and Bob have a wonderful secret."

Julie's face lit up. "Oh, Allen! Really?"

Allen nodded. "But don't say anything yet. Let *them* tell you."

Finally, after they were well on their way, Allen spoke. "Say, kids—uh—didn't you have something to tell Julie?"

Silence—but not for long. "Oh, did *we* have something to tell her?" Sandra spoke with that I'm-dying-to-tell-you tone in her voice.

"Yes," Bob echoed, "did *we* have something to tell—"

Julie could hardly hold back the smiles. "Oh, come on, you two!"

Sandra giggled. "Really, Julie. What *else* is new?"

Now Julie looked, mockingly stern, at her "big brother." Bob looked first at Allen and "little sis" and then at Sandra as he gave her a squeeze and sighed, "My Sandra and me—we're engaged!"

Hearty congratulations were in order, of course. The engagement had to be secret—for a while, at least—but it was very, very special....

Allen had driven as fast as he deemed safe, but just as they pulled into the station at two minutes to seven, they watched helplessly as the big bus pulled out. Now, what to do?

"Let's catch it in San Martino!" Sandra exclaimed. "It always stops there." So, they were off to San Martino, another 14 miles away. "Panic time" was the word of the hour. No one knew just how long the bus would stop or how long the line would be at the ticket window, nor on just exactly what corner the depot was located. Was it Main or Market?

And in San Martino, city of one-way streets, did they take 7th or 8th Street to get there? If Bob missed the bus tonight—although Bob would have loved spending another night in Riverdale—it would mean a loss of time and money to him.

Arriving, at long last, at the bus station in San Martino, each breathed a sigh of relief as they saw the bus was still there. Bob rushed in to buy his ticket, while the other three unloaded his belongings. When they had carried his luggage into the depot, Bob greeted them with a half-wry, wouldn't-you-know-it smile. "Guess what. My bus doesn't leave here until (groan) 8:50!"

This meant a few extra moments for the young lovers, and they made the most of it, thinking and talking and planning the months ahead. Just before 8:30, Sandra and Bob slipped outside for only a minute or two. And, to this day, only Bob Miller, Sandra Lee, and God know the goodbye that they whispered in that special moment.... Then shaking hands with Allen and squeezing his "sis" Julie, Bob bade his dearest friends goodbye.

The road back was long, but Sandra's face seemed to be radiantly alive. Once home in the stillness of her own room, Sandra could relax and think of the happenings of the day, of the past week, of the past year, and of the future years. She closed her eyes. Bob loved her, she loved him, and they both loved God, which was more important than anything else.

Mommie had gone to heaven, and Daddy and she would make the best of everything. God loved them; He knew best. Opening her eyes slightly, Sandra could see from her pillow, in the glow of the hall nightlight, Bob's picture and the little white box she had placed so tenderly beside it. She reached for it. And clutching her Christmas valentine to her heart, she closed her eyes again and softly drifted into dreamland.

What Love Makes Right

This is a first-person reflection of an unidentified protagonist about an unmarried twin sister who has given birth to a baby. The writer marvels at how easily it could have been her. Is it based, however loosely, on actual events that Julie may have observed, no matter how remotely? Or is it an expression of some sort of duality in Julie's personality?

PART 1. GROWING UP Together

There she is—see over there on the mantel—my sister. She's my twin; would you believe it? Her senior picture is there by mine. Look at her eyes, those warm brown ones. That's the only physical trait we've always shared. Right now, it seems as if she could speak to me.

"Kathy! Kathy! Get out of bed—it's morning," she would playfully scream at me. But—today—the room is empty and silent. Donna's gone. I missed her terribly at first. But let me start at the beginning.

When we were very little girls, people could never tell us apart. We dressed alike, talked alike, even laughed alike. And we were always so very close. We shared everything—dolls, dresses, crayons.

I remember how it was in school, especially when we played piano duets. We loved to constantly switch parts. Nobody ever knew who was playing what. Our family put us on a pedestal. We always went to the school parties; everyone missed us if we weren't there.

It's hard to say when the change came creeping into our innocently beautiful and happy lives. I suppose the first thing was when our golden brown locks changed color. By some strange quirk of nature, Donna's hair took on a slightly auburn tinge while my own gradually darkened to this deep umber hue you see I have now.

Until about eighth grade, we had both been skinny little kids. Soon we both gained weight, but Donna did a bit more than I did. Suddenly she took a growth spurt, and most strangers thought she was my *older* sister. She was so full of life and vigor, while I sat most of the time buried in my books.

Maybe it was good that our interests took different directions. The first year of high school divided us even further. Suddenly she grew very scientific. Electronics. Our music, however, seemed to be the one thing with which I was the happiest. Still, we had those long intimate talks that only sisters know. We shared the same mutual feelings and ideas as we always had. We seemed to understand each other so completely.

Then we met Tom. As far as I could tell, he was an ordinary guy. He could have been the pastor's son, or a mechanic's boy, or even a well-disciplined orphan—any one of a number of the kind of guys who attended our high school.

But to Donna he was different. From the very first, she never doubted him for a moment. I still remember how excited she was that night of her first date with him. Of course, I was just as eager to know exactly what happened. I was surprised and flattered that Donna confided in me. By this time, I had almost come to *feel* like a younger sister (which indeed I was, having been born six minutes after Donna). Yet Donna and I were still inseparable. And the more she told me about Tom, the more *I* liked him, too.

Now, like our coloring books and arithmetic and piano playing, we shared Tom. Donna went on all the dates with him, but I did the scheming and planning and counseling. I felt I knew Tom as well as she did; after all, she told me everything. Like was exciting and adventurous.

Then something strange happened in Donna. Tom began dating around. I thought it was only normal for a 16-year-old guy. But somehow Donna didn't feel that way. I tried to convince her that if she and Tom were really meant for each other, he'd come back to her. And he did—occasionally. That wasn't enough for her.

I tried to get *her* to date around, too. *My* current was Pete, and I was having the ball of my life. Donna and I just didn't understand each other anymore. It hurt, slowly and intangibly. Even our common interests seemed to grow less and less. I was on a secretarial fling while Donna stayed buried in her chemistry—and brooded over Tom.

But time proved that Donna might be right, and I had been wrong. Ironically, our physical appearance grew more alike as it once had been. We weighed exactly the same, had the same body measurements. Our hair, although slightly different shades, was very similar in style. Even our glasses were identical. And once more our personalities converged. I understood, as never before, how deeply Donna felt about Tom. In fact, I almost envied her.

Tom went away to school, far enough away that he and Donna could only see each other once every several weeks. But it didn't seem to matter. They wrote frequently.

"Tom and I are in love," she announced blissfully one day. "It's for *real* this time, Kathy!"

I believed her. She seemed to sparkle so. Tom was growing up. Every word he spoke, every kiss they shared, every letter he wrote—I knew it all so well. Donna shared her wildest dreams with me only, her sister. They had talked of the future, of their marriage, their ministry for God—together. It seemed as if no love could have been more perfect. I, too, looked forward to her greatest happiness.

PART 2. GRADUATION

Soon we were lost in the whirl of our graduation. It was so beautiful; we both cried. But the excitement of college life soon caught us up. I remember those warm summer afternoons we spent window shopping for bedspreads and rugs and curtains and hoping that we would get a nice dormitory room.

The college was immense—and all the people! There was registration, orientation, new classes, new teachers, new friends—and a third roommate. She was a lovely girl, Diana. She and Donna had so much in common. By now Donna had been taken by my previous secretarial ambitions while my major was going to be piano. Diana, too, was going to be a secretary. Besides, she was in love with Steve.

I tried harder than ever to not interfere with Donna's life—only to help her if I could. But as the weeks passed, we became strangers again. Night after night Diana and Donna shared their shorthand and accounting and then shared their Steve and Tom. They did not include me in those intimate conversations. I was always supposed to be asleep in my bunk.

But I wasn't a social wallflower. I dated—more than I ever had in my life. I was so thrilled with *all* of college life, from the most routine class work to the exotic Spring Banquet. But, because I wasn't "in love," I "couldn't understand how it was," I heard them whisper once. For a while, I ignored it. Of *course,* I understood my own twin sister. Of *course,* I knew what it was like to be in love—Donna had told me.

Then I listened more closely to their conversations—those Saturday nights when they didn't even seem to know I was around. Diana's ideas were so different from the ones Donna and I had always shared. I could see how Diana felt about men and love and marriage and children—yet I never could quite agree with her.

And I *didn't* understand my very own sister, how she had changed. No, we never quarreled violently as we once had about Tom—not one disgruntled word. I dared not say a thing. I tried to blame Diana for the influence she was having on my sister. I tried to hide from myself what I knew deep inside—that it was Donna herself who was pushing me so rudely from her life. But, proud and naïve, I only wondered and waited.

"Sex is a perfectly normal part of genuine love," I would hear in the wee morning hours as I lay still and listened to the two voices in my room. I soon gathered that Diana always went out with Steve on Saturday nights to a secluded little haven of their own. It was near the college, some place called Rainbow Rock. Soon Donna and Tom, when he came home, found one for themselves at Willow Creek. "I love him very much and have never loved another man, nor will ever love any other man like this. In God's sight, we do belong to each other."

Donna and Diana both seemed so happy, so contented, so convinced that love, as they experienced it, was right. "If we didn't love each other so completely, of course, it would be wrong. But we *do* love each other only—forever and ever, amen—and we both love God. This kind of love makes it right."

One night, when even *my* curiosity was to the bursting point, Diana filled Donna in on the details of the most complete act of physical love. Even I listened intently, wondering and thinking. "Take it from me," Diana concluded, "*never* say you'll never do it. Because if you love him, you will."

I thought very fleetingly of my own relationships with any of the fellows I had been dating. Not in my wildest imagination could I picture myself "doing it." Nor could I picture it happening to Tom and Donna. I wanted desperately somehow to stop her before it was too late. Yet, how could I convince her she was wrong? *Love makes it right.*

Summer came. Diana and Steve disappeared into memory. Tom came home. I had never seen my sister happier. Tom would be at the college the very next fall. Once again, Donna and I seemed as close as we ever had been. She assured me that Diana's "influence" hadn't been bad, that her own love for Tom was her own choice. And I'm sure it was.

I'll never forget that sultry September day just two weeks before school was to begin when Donna and I went downtown. She had put our biggest suitcase into the car. "Lock is broken," she told me. Has to be repaired. We talked eagerly of the coming year back at college—at least

I did. I didn't notice her strange quietness while we window shopped together as we always had done.

Then we stopped at the bank. I supposed she was going to deposit her last paycheck in the small account that Mom and Dad had started for each of us when we were small children. How could I have known her account would be empty when she returned? Before I knew what was happening, Donna pulled the car up beside a large gray building.

"Help me with the suitcase, will you, Kathy?" Her voice quivered slightly.

Bewildered and amused, I reached for the empty luggage to find it heavy. She tugged on it, too, and we carried it inside. My head was spinning as I stood there speechless, watching her buy a bus ticket. Surely this was a joke of some sort. Some red-capped boy even came, put a tag on the suitcase, and carried it away.

"It leaves in five minutes." She smiled weirdly.

"Okay, sis, I give up. What are you up to?" I giggled.

She sat down on the worn bench. "I'm just going up to Aunt Margaret's for a little while." Her voice was casually soft.

"Aunt Margaret's!" Funny, we had always taken our vacations together before. "But school starts a week from Monday—"

Suddenly her solemn gaze froze my words in mid-air. She spoke slowly and deliberately. "I won't be going back to college with you this year, Kathy. I can't—I'm pregnant."

I was stunned! I tried to laugh. "Oh, I see. Tom's going to meet you, and you'll have the wedding there, then—"

She shook her head slowly as her glassy eyes stared far past the big bus that was just pulling in. "There will not be any wedding, Kathy. Not now—not ever. Tom will be there at college this year. His parents want him to be a teacher, you know."

"But I also know you *love* each other!" I protested.

"Tom's a stranger to me. We don't love each other now. We haven't for a long time." Her voice was bitter. "All I've been to him is a sex partner!"

"Oh, Donna, don't say that!" My voice was choked with emotion. "Why did it have to happen to *you,* my own sister?"

Her sad eyes looked deep into my tear-filled ones. "It didn't *have* to happen." She placed a sympathizing hand on my trembling arm. "And it won't have to happen to *you,* Kathy! Love is good and right when it stays pure. But somehow" —she bit her lip— "it didn't work for Tom and me. Oh, Kathy, don't *ever* do what I did!" She squeezed my arm hard. "Don't *ever* do it!"

PART 3. TRYING TO UNDERSTAND

"Donna, how—you—my sister—why—why?!" was all I could say as the tears streamed down my face. Tom and Donna had planned so much. She had built her entire life and future around him. Now that was all over. Her whole world had collapsed. I couldn't believe it. In silence, we walked out to the bus.

At last, I could speak again. "Wh-what are you going to do?" I whispered painfully.

She shrugged. "Have an illegitimate baby, what else? It doesn't really matter anymore." She turned toward me with a tired smile. "Kathy, take up where I left off—and don't make my mistakes. We've been so close for so many years. But I'm leaving you now. It's *got* to be this way. Do you understand that, Kathy?"

I swallowed hard. "Donna—my sister—why?!" I sobbed. In that single moment, I seemed to remember all we had shared through the past 18 years—even Tom. I nodded reluctantly.

She kissed my cheek just before she bounded up the stairs into the bus. Then, turning sharply, she spoke the last words I ever heard her say. "By the way, if you ever see Diana and Steve again, give them my *regards!*"

The sting in the sarcasm was too much. I fled to the car and lay there sobbing violently for a long while.

That fateful day when Donna left was nearly a year ago. So much has happened since then. Sure, they asked about Donna back at school. "She's back east this year," I told them. They didn't ask many questions—it's a big college, lots of people. I told her friends—our friends—enough to satisfy them. I guess no one else really knew how things had been between her and Tom—no one except Diana and Steve—and they hadn't been around for a long time.

I tried my best to forget the hurt. I had a wonderful roommate, Linda—lively, full of fun, soon to be married. I knew Donna would have liked her, too. Yet, far into the year, memories of Donna and all she could have become haunted me day and night.

Yes, Tom was there on campus. Not once did he even *ask* about Donna, even though he made it a point to speak to me every time he saw me. He must have known how much it hurt me just to see him and be reminded of what he had done to Donna.

Early in the spring, just about when I thought the baby was almost due, I sent a small parcel of baby things. Within a week, I received a thank you note—the only time Donna has ever written—along with a picture of little Todd. It pained me deeply to see how much the infant resembled Tom's baby pictures. Yet, the child looked much like Donna, too—and like her twin sister. I marveled in sadness at how close we had been—and how easily it *could* have been me in Donna's place! And I breathed a silent prayer for us both.

I tried so hard to not hate Tom. He sent her money once. But he never saw his own baby—never even wanted to. At home, I found all the things—letters, dried-up flowers, empty candy box and perfume bottles—that Tom had ever given Donna. I wanted to burn everything. But I was Donna's faithful twin sister. Someday—somehow—wouldn't Donna come back? So, I buried it all deep in the back of our closet.

I *did* determine to not make the same mistakes Donna had. I determined to take up where she had left off. She was going to have a brilliant career—traveling, meeting people, eventually marrying and having a home. Yet Donna had fallen in love. How can *I* ever love a man the way Donna did?

Today I went to a wedding—Diana and Steve's. When she saw me, she mentioned in passing that she was *so* sorry to hear about little Todd, and wouldn't Donna and Tom get married, anyway? But she and Steve were so lost in their own inexpressible happiness. As I watched them leave the church arm in arm, I imagined for a fleeting moment that it could have been Donna and Tom.

Things are so perfect for Diana and Steve. They have spent five years being in love. This, their wedding day, is the fulfillment of all their hopes. They have built their future around each other. They have shared their dreams from the beginning and now will *always* share them—forever and ever, amen. They had had a lot in common with Donna and Tom. They loved in the same way. They did the same sort of things. And somehow love had made it right for them.

The silent bitterness crept up when I thought again of my own sister—so alone now, so forgotten by Tom, the father of her baby. Suddenly she seemed so far away, so divorce from my life. I don't know how long I must have stood there in the reception hall, watching the guests, gazing through all the joy and excitement, yet not really seeing anything at all.

Then I found my arms around Diana. She was such a beautiful bride and so radiantly happy. I even squeezed Steve's hand. "Best regards!" I whispered—and I meant it sincerely.

"Kathy." Diana spoke my name the way she used to speak Donna's—she really had thought so much of her. "Do come and see us sometime," she invited. "And bring George."

George! Yes, George. I met him at school last year. We have had a beautiful friendship. It was the music we mutually love that drew us together. It seems no one can really understand my deepest feelings like George can. But Donna felt that way about Tom, too. And Diana feels this way about Steve.

As far as I can tell, George is an ordinary guy. He could be the pastor's son, or a mechanic's boy, or even a well-disciplined orphan—any one of a number of the kind of guys who attend our school. How can I believe *he's* different?

From the very first, I *have* doubted. George *is* a wonderful person—but so were Tom and Steve. And, like Tom and Steve, he is a man with all the capacity for living and loving—and hurting. What if I, a woman like Donna and Diana, respond to life itself? What if I, too—against all my pure and prudish intentions—fall in love with George?

How can *I,* Donna's twin sister and Diana's friend, *know* what love makes right?

Rendezvous

This short story in two parts is about Howard Davidson, the love of Julie's life whom she meets in the fall of 1964 during her sophomore year at La Paloma College. It is set in some future time after Howard's graduation from college and his embarking on a concert artist career. Actually, it's a fantasy written by Julie Scott in 1967, during her first year of marriage to Howard Davidson.

PREPARING FOR THE CONCERT

The keys jingled in the dim foyer, along with the sound of approaching footsteps. In a moment, the massive oak doors creaked open. Mr. Howard Davidson, with his companion, stepped out into the bright sunshine. He gazed upward for a long moment at the majestic white stone building from where he had come. He could see the tall chamber that stretched toward the sky. He still pictured the great console inside.

"Tired?" The girl's voice struck the still air.

The man nodded slightly. "One more rehearsal day, Julie, and then..."

"A wonderful concert," she added, "by a marvelous artist."

He smiled, his eyes still fixed on the immense structure before him. "It's a fabulous organ." Together they started toward Howard's little red Volkswagen, which was almost lost in the late afternoon shadow of Carnegie Hall.

It was rush hour in New York City, yet Howard Davidson hardly saw the busy streets or heard the honking about him. His mind drifted back as he remembered how this had all begun.

It was in Phoenix—his own city. Even now, he sensed the breathless silence of the desert cathedral before his hands ever played a note. He felt the thrill of the keyboard as the sounds from the giant pipes filled the church and floated out into the summer night. But it hadn't stopped there. After San Francisco, there had been Dallas, and then—

"The Chicago concert," the girl's voice filtered into his reminiscence, "—how does that organ compare with this one?"

"Well, the Chicago organ had a better selection of reed stops, but this one has ten more ranks of pipes. However," he went on, "I've never seen such an acoustically responsive auditorium as—"

"Pardon me, Mr. Davidson," Julie broke in, "but we just passed the hotel."

With a chuckle, he turned the car at the next intersection. He still basked in the memories of the wild ovation in Miami and the fan letters from Los Angeles and Denver. And now—his biggest chance—he would perform in New York. Success here meant success of the entire concert tour.

"Thank you." Julie stepped out of the car when they pulled up to the front door.

"I must make a few more calls—president of the A.G.O., *New York Times* editor," he commented briefly. "See you later."

That night in the hotel, Howard stopped by the pay phone in the lobby. He unfolded the slip of paper that he drew from his pocket. "Call Janie—Cherry 4-9761," it read. After dialing with a slow, steady hand, he waited.

"Hello?" The woman's voice seemed unsuspecting.

"Hello. This is Howard Davidson calling. I received a message this morning to call—"

"Howard!" she cried in sheer delight. "How *are* you?"

"Fine, Janie." He smiled. "Never thought I would talk to you in New York City! Are you living here now?"

"No," she replied, "just vacationing. I just *happened* to see the announcement in the morning paper for your concert tomorrow night. They gave the name of your hotel, but I wasn't sure the message would get to you."

Howard chuckled. "Well, will I see you before we both leave town? You'll be at Carnegie tomorrow night?"

"You bet I will!" she assured him. "And if I can fight my way through the crowds—"

"I'll be looking for you, Janie." Howard pictured the scene.

"The French have a word for it, don't they?" Her voice was almost mysterious.

"Oh—*rendezvous*?" He chuckled. "Tomorrow night, Janie."

"Goodbye, Howard," she murmured, "until then."

Howard slept little that night. His music lay undisturbed on the desk close beside him, but Howard tossed and turned. Every hum of the elevator outside his room seemed to Howard like the surging wind past the huge shutters of the organ. Every onrush of traffic was a sudden *sforzando* of the 32-foot pedal notes. Every whisper of wind brought the ethereal flutes and strings from high above Howard's whirling brain. Every moonbeam was a great staff pushing the half notes, the quarter notes, the dotted eighths and sixteenths that filled his weary body.

Morning came at last. Howard was already in the parking lot when he realized Julie was not with him. Then he saw her slight frame leaning on his car.

"You're late," she said politely. "Weren't we to leave at nine?"

"I'm sorry." He hung his head. Then, "Hey, what are you doing out *here*? I mean, why did you come out—"

Julie laughed. "I knew you were deep in contemplation," she said. "You *have* been for several days. Anyway, it was such a lovely morning for a walk. So I just ended it here."

He opened her door. "I'm so glad you understand."

With a click, he snapped open his briefcase. "Check the music, will you, please?"

"Yes, sir!" Methodically, Julie lifted the stacks of music from the tan leather bag and, with secretarial efficiency, soon had everything in complete order. "Relax!" she commanded gently, looking at his tensed physique. "You know it all so well."

He took a deep breath as one hand fell from the steering wheel to shift gears. "Just the *thought* of tonight!" he stared straight ahead. "Julie, do you realize what it can mean to a musician's career!"

"Yes," she replied softly, "I know."

The empty auditorium was almost cold that July morning as Howard's skilled hands and feet called forth the powers of the greatest masters that had ever lived—Bach, Buxtehude, Franck. Although she had heard his repertoire many times, Julie stood wide-eyed and entranced, never moving a muscle except to turn the pages as Howard had beckoned. After all, that's what she was there to do.

Hour after hour passed. Boellman. Handel. Mozart. Sowerby. Hindemith. It was well past one o'clock that warm afternoon when Howard and Julie seated themselves in a small sidewalk café called *The Rendezvous.* The food was excellent, but Howard ate very little.

At long last he spoke. "The Organ Concerto in E-flat," he said dreamily, as Julie nodded slightly. "How would it sound with the orchestra parts on a Steinway or Yamaha grand?"

She looked at him with an almost amused curiosity. "Might sound all right. Probably sound *better* with an orchestra."

His deep blue eyes pierced through her seemingly complacent countenance. "But we *could* work it up in a few months' time—don't you think?"

"Could be, perhaps," Julie agreed. Then, with a twinkle, "You can't afford an orchestra, Mr. Davidson?"

"And you, *too*?" He smiled condescendingly.

There was a long moment of silence. The neon sign above the café, visible from their table, kept flashing on and off. *Rendezvous. Rendezvous.*

"Tonight!" Howard breathed half out loud. His gaze shot far past the milling crowds. "Just thinking of—of the future," he mused, "and all it could mean."

During the rest of the afternoon, Howard tried to relax as much as possible, but it was difficult in view of the big event that every moment brought closer and closer. He stretched out on a lounge by the pool and buried himself in the latest issues of *The Organ Journal* Julie had so thoughtfully brought. It was a lazy day, but he seemed to absorb little of the casual atmosphere that surrounded him. For a fleeting moment he thought of his pupils in California—those ambitious young organ students, so promising but so untrained as he once had been. He even thought once of visiting the museum at Carnegie—the Music Hall of Fame. At last, he dozed—his contorted body started to unwind—as the sun sank lower in the sultry sky.

Presently Julie appeared with a cool glass of lemonade. "They will serve supper in half an hour," she announced.

He looked blankly for a long moment into her innocent brown eyes. "Thank you," he said.

AFTER THE CONCERT

By seven-thirty nearly three-quarters of the auditorium was filled. It was not the first time Howard had seen so many people. He didn't even pace back and forth in his dressing room this time. Calmly, he stood to answer the faint knock on his door.

"Julie!" He spoke in mild rebuke.

"They're waiting for you," she said. "The music is ready, Prof."

Her adoring look made him swell with well-earned pride. "You're a great page turner," he whispered as he rushed past her onto the open stage where an explosion of applause awaited him.

Julie, dressed in black satin, was barely visible behind the great organ and tuxedo-clad artist except as her functional hand reached out to turn a page. Magnificent was the music that poured forth from Howard's hands and feet and heart! Like the roar of a thunderstorm, like the ethereal depths of an exotic sea, like the quiet charm of a Gothic cathedral—Howard gave all this, and more, to the spellbound audience. The time passed quickly, and the response was tremendous. Women threw flowers; the men cheered. They all gave him a standing ovation as Howard came back for bow after bow and encore after encore. Julie, almost misty, had taken the briefcase of music and headed backstage.

Howard grew tired as he signed autograph after autograph. It was a long time before the crowd of eager fans thinned out. Even the appearance of the heavy-set, stern-faced custodian who stood close by the organ with folded arms seemed to have little effect on dispersing the crowd.

As the tower clock in the distance was striking the hour, Howard turned to leave. It was then that he saw her. He peered through the dimly lighted hall until she was close enough to speak.

"Janie! You came."

"Yes, Howard. I said I would." With a white-gloved hand, she gave him her program to sign. "You were absolutely terrific!"

He smiled humbly as his trembling hand grasped the pen. Slowly, he handed it back to her as their eyes met for the first time in many years. He could see how the city light that diffused through a high rose window fell on her golden hair. "Janie," he said at last, "it's been so long."

She nodded. "I always knew you'd make good, Howard. I remember how it was in school—"

"Ah, yes." His mind drifted back across fond memories. He chuckled. "Remember how the kids always gave poor old Mr. Harris a bad time? Just because he was bald—"

She giggled. "Then there was the time we went with the class on that picnic. And guess who got lost!"

"Say, that was really when it all started, wasn't it?"

There was a silent pause.

Janie glanced absentmindedly at the now silent organ. "I'll never forget that banquet—and the music."

"Then there was the party at Larsons'—the very last one when—w-we thought we'd never see each other again."

"Tell me, Howard, you graduated from that university in California, didn't you?"

"Just a couple of years ago," he answered sheepishly. "I had a rough go of it at first."

"But you've got what it takes—determination *and* talent. I always admired that, Howard."

"And you, Janie, you were working for Dr. Hutchins in Ludington when I saw you last. Did you finish at Michigan State? I remember the big plans we used to talk about—"

"I did," she replied, "just a few years after—after we said goodbye. But I'm teaching now—in Ludington."

"Teaching! Janie, I'm proud of you."

"I'm proud of *you,* Howard. You know that. From the first day we stayed after school and I listened to you play the little spinet in the Ludington Cafeteria—"

Just then, a toddler's exclamation echoed through the stillness. "There she is, Daddy!" And a tall, dark stranger stepped out of the shadows with a curly headed little girl in his arms.

"Honey, this is Mr. Davidson, the organist," Janie said as she took the wriggling bundle into her own arms. "Howard, I'd like you to meet my husband, Floyd Wright, and our little Debbie."

As the two men shook hands and exchanged greetings, a door from the hallway opened and Howard spotted a familiar form. He grasped her hand. "And *this* is the girl I could never have gotten through the concert without! Julie, I'd like you to meet the Wrights—Floyd, Janie, and—"

"Debbie," Mr. Wright smiled. "Nice to meet you both."

"Next year," Janie inserted, "you two must include Ludington in your itinerary."

The man beside her nodded politely. "Best wishes, Mr. Davidson—and Julie!" Then he turned, with his wife and child, to leave.

"Janie Wright," Howard whispered in awe when the darkness had enveloped them.

"So—*that's* Janie!" Julie's voice was teasing.

"Yeah." Howard laughed with her. "She still remembered who I was."

"Hmm." Julie seemed unconcerned. "Say, the A.G.O. president talked to me—he couldn't get through to you for the people! Anyway, he already wants to know about next year. I told him you'd write when we get back to California. But what *about* next year, Howard?"

He slipped his arm around her and planted a kiss on her forehead. "Together!" he said deliberately. "You and me—piano *and* organ. There's the E-Flat Concerto for a start—"

"Oh, Howard!" She responded to his embrace. "Do you *really* think I can—we can—do it?"

"Darling,"—he squeezed her suddenly— "you're a pianist, remember?"

"But something this *big*—"

"Hey, we're a team now, don't forget." He stroked her hair lightly. "Besides, I love you *and* our music."

"We'll do it, sweetheart—together."

She closed her eyes and laid her head against his broad shoulder. "I'll never regret the day we became a team."

"Neither will I!" he sighed softly. "Come on, Mrs. Davidson, we've got a big day ahead—Carnegie Museum, lunch at *The Rendezvous*, and a long trip home."

Journey Home

This is a mysterious first-person story, deliberately written to read as if it were the last chapter of a long novel. It was written during the winter of 1969, considerably later than the other Riverdale stories, and really has nothing at all to do with Riverdale. Or does it?...

I REMEMBER THE NIGHT well. It was blistering cold, and the wind whipped the snow savagely around the old brick house. The fire burned low on the hearth, but I was not warm inside. I had paced restlessly across the big hooked rug as the eerie flames flickered my already trembling shadow onto the gray wall behind me.

But now I sat quietly and gazed through the slitted curtains for a long while. I knew the moon would have been shining across the snow-blanketed countryside had the clouds not pressed so thickly to the earth. Now there was no moon, no stars—only the moan of a lonely wind through the naked trees.

Suddenly, the boy burst into the room. He was covered with melting snow from head to foot. In the light of the red lantern he carried, I noticed his reddened cheeks and bright blue eyes.

"Missy Lora?" He gave me a shy, questioning look as he held out a black-gloved hand. "Dees fo' you, mum!"

Wordlessly, I took the unwelcome envelope.

From somewhere in the back room, I heard the housemaster call in his low friendly manner, "Come, Sonny, have a bit of hot tea before going on." And the boy disappeared as quickly as he had come.

In choking silence, I tore open the letter. It was brief. Although I had been half expecting it, somehow it was unbelievingly stinging. I felt as if a great bony hand had suddenly closed in around me. I wanted to scream or run—or something. But I stood numbed in front of the fire. Almost without thinking, I tossed in the crumpled pages.

Just then the housemaster came into the room. I must have started when I heard his footsteps, for he asked me, "Something troubling you, Missy?"

I turned, but I could not speak. I stared far past him, trying to imagine what might happen to me now. Hurriedly, I left the room.

"There's still some hot tea in the kitchen," he called up the stairs after me. "Do get a good night's sleep, Missy!"

I went into my room, but I knew I could not obey. I looked around quickly. The place was tidy, its furnishings few. But my eyes fell upon the table. Just where I had left it earlier that day lay the ring. For a speechless moment that seemed like an eternity, it held me spellbound. A thousand thoughts rushed in and out of my mind. I saw the summer days by the lake, and the green forest with its deep, sweet peace. I knew it was all over, and I could hold back no longer.

My head was spinning as I slipped the ring onto my hand. Then, before I knew what I was doing, I was outside. The sharp chill must have temporarily brought me halfway to my senses. The wind had subsided, but the night was bitterly cold.

I stumbled on through the snow. The tears were streaming down my cheeks by this time. Twice I brushed a frozen salty bead of water from my chin. I was tired, very tired, but at last I reached the forest. It looked so different from the last time I had been there—last autumn just as the leaves had begun to turn. Now there seemed to be only a skimpy mass of rough crooked sticks protruding from the white expanse of snow.

With what seemed like my last ounce of energy, I made my way to the cave at the foot of the hill. It wasn't a cave, really, just a big hollow in the rock where we had spent many hours together with the warm breezes playing around us.

The cave was empty, but it seemed to shelter me somewhat from the cold. I looked down at my hands and tried to move them. I brought first one then the other to my ears then to my nose. I felt nothing. But the ring on my finger looked shiny, almost new again. My tears had stopped. I felt the day had drained me of all that I could be. My blind frustration was turning into stolid indifference. I felt strangely warm and sleepy all over....

I don't know how long I lay in the snow before they came and took me back to the house. I only remember waking in a dim yellow room and a soft bed. The door creaked slightly, and I saw the boy again, standing there. He wore the same shy look as he ventured inside. I felt angry, but only for a moment. I must have smiled then, for he smiled, too.

"How you feel, Missy?" He came over to my side.

"Wh-where am I, Sonny?" My voice sounded hoarse and funny.

"In your room." He seemed puzzled. "Dee houseman, he carry you back from woods. I fin' yo' dar in snow last night and..." His proud words trailed off as he searched my face for some response.

"Sonny." I had gained control of my words by this time. "Don't you think I should leave—I mean, go someplace, away from here?"

"But not in blizzard, Missy!" His blue eyes widened.

I laughed roughly. "Tell me, Sonny, today the housemaster goes into the city to market, hey?"

"Oh, yes, mum! He prepare carriage now."

"Then, run! Tell him I'm going with him today. Hurry, now; I must get ready!"

He stared at me for a long moment, then turned and scurried awkwardly out. Sonny wouldn't have understood any more of an explanation.

The sun was shining when I walked out of the house, my belongings tucked away in the two small bags that I carried. I breathed deeply. Snow glistened along the path to the stables. Sonny was helping fasten the horses when they saw me.

"Well, Missy, what are you taking to market today?" The housemaster laughed good-naturedly as he took my bags and tossed them lightly into the carriage. I laughed, too, and took his hand as he helped me in. Neither of us spoke of the night before.

When he had seated himself at the reins, I spoke—half to him, half to Sonny who still stood by with the same puzzlement as ever. "I am leaving today," I announced bravely. "I've—I've been here a long time. I must go. It wouldn't be the same for me here anymore, you know..."

There was a long, tense silence. "Well," the housemaster's quiet voice broke in, "it is your decision, Missy."

"I loved it here, really!" I was choked with emotion. "Your lakes, your forest, your skies—even your snow. Especially your house." I looked at the old man beside me. He said nothing; only a pleased, gentle half-smile crossed his wrinkled face.

"I—I can't stay, not now." I looked toward Sonny—I had to—I felt his uninterrupted gaze upon me, this mysterious strange-acting woman.

He bit his lip. "We mees you, mum!"

Suddenly, I grabbed my hand and jerked off the ring. At once I held it out toward the boy. "From Missy," I said.

Without a word, he took it. In return, he gave me a look I shall never forget.

The horses neighed impatiently. "Goodbye, Sonny." The words were barely audible. "Tell them—tell them that I'm going home. And the carriage was gone.

Where Are They Now?

At the time of this writing (in 2021), Juliana Harvard's research reveals:

Allen Macintosh did not become a minister but became interested in the broadcasting industry. He married Shirley, a nurse, and they have two grown children. Allen and Shirley lived in southern California where he was Senior Manager of a prominent Christian radio station. He is now divorced from Shirley and married to a classmate he knew at San Margo Academy and, at last contact with Julie, was in the insurance industry. He is not on Facebook.

Bill Johnson became an integral part of Julie's inner circle of friends in Riverdale for a short time. He left to join the Army; and when he came back, he married Annie, his older brother's step-daughter in North Carolina. They are still married, with two grown children, Bill Jr. and Tina. Bill and Annie Johnson became grandparents and live in southern California. Bill had a career in computers until his retirement and maintained contact with Sandra throughout the years. Sandra recently found him on Facebook.

Billy Kingston was killed in a hunting accident before he reached his 20th birthday.

Bob Miller did not become a minister but went into teaching instead. He became a computer genius long before desktop PCs became popular. He is still married to Sandra Lee and taught computing at a high school for gifted students until his retirement. Bob and Sandra are grandparents and great-grandparents and live in southern California.

Bruce Donaldson became a dentist and was on Facebook as of July 2019.

Carolyn Bullenhacker disappeared from Riverdale, but Julie found her on Facebook in 2012. She did not respond to Julie's Friend request.

Cynthia Donaldson became a pediatric nurse. She married but did not have children. She lives in the northwest. She is on Facebook and accepted Julie's Facebook Friend request but does not display her photo.

Darlene Steele is one of the few who still lived in Riverdale. She married, had a daughter, and is now divorced. She is not actually Julie's sister, but was a very close friend. Julie once found Darlene's daughter on Facebook, who said she was estranged from her mother and could not give Julie any current information about her. Sadly, Julie has lost contact with Darlene.

Dennis Holman is married, but no further information is available. Julie found him on Facebook in 2012.

Dick Clarke is a fictional character who does not exist, but someone based loosely on a childhood friend whose father was a dentist in Riverdale. Julie found him on Facebook in 2012.

Eddy Kingston moved from Riverdale but lived in southern California for several years. No other information was available until Julie found him on Facebook shortly before his death in a plane crash in 2016. At that time, his elderly mother **Norma** was still alive. Julie says, "He was a father of six children, retired from his own company (Kingston & Sons), pilot, and drummer. He had just celebrated his 70th birthday when he was killed in a plane crash in northern Idaho. We had just connected on Facebook within the last year."

Ella Hargrove married a successful business executive, and they had four daughters. She and her husband still live in southern California. Ella is on Facebook.

Eloise Tibbs disappeared for many years, but Julie recently found her on Facebook. Julie also became Facebook friends with Eloise's younger brother **Chuck,** who was born after the Tibbs family moved from Riverdale.

Frank Hargrove joined the Army and is now deceased. He and Carlos remained lifelong friends until Frank's death. No further information is available. **Carlos** lives in Oceanview and is active on Facebook.

Howard Davidson and Julie Scott were married between their junior and senior years at La Paloma College, and were divorced seven years later when Howard came out as a gay man. A few years after that, Howard moved to San Francisco, where he is a popular organ performer and composer. He has been senior staff organist at The Castro Theatre since 1978. He is now married to his partner whom he has been with since 1993.

Jim Donaldson studied medicine at the University of Mexico and became a medical doctor. To those who knew him as a child who was frequently labeled "sissy" because of his mannerisms, it was no surprise to learn that he was gay. Unfortunately, he died of AIDS many years ago.

JoAnn Cunningham... No information is available.

Joe Lee is a fictional character who does not exist in real life.

Judy Hargrove.... No information is available, but Julie says she found her on Facebook once.

Julie Scott married Howard Davidson and was devastated when their seven-year marriage ended after he came out as a gay man. She then married an Air Force man (at which time she became Juliana Harvard), had two children, and was divorced after 20 years (at which time she legally became Juliana Davidson again, but still prefers to use her pen name of Juliana Harvard when writing her stories). During that time, she came out as a lesbian, and she and her teenage daughter moved to California to live with her partner (**Lina Jackson Reiter**) in the San Francisco Bay Area. They were legally married in 2013. She has occasional contact with Howard, who is still her best friend and soulmate on a very esoteric level. Julie has three grandsons and three step-grandchildren.

Ken Nelson remained married to Rebecca, they had two children, and they became grandparents. They still lived in southern California, in a neighboring town to Riverdale, until Ken's death in 2018 at age 74. His obituary says, "He retired from Riverdale Municipal Water District after 30 years. He loved trucks, tractors, travel, and time with family."

Kenny Macintosh... No further information is available, but he was on Facebook in 2012.

Kurt Gaston became a successful minister and professor, earned his doctorate, and got married to a beautiful French Canadian woman. They have two grown children and grandchildren. They lived and worked in a foreign mission field until they retired to Michigan. He is on Facebook but rarely posts.

LeRoy Chester disappeared from Sandra's life, but Sandra thinks she found him on Facebook.

Marsha... No further information is available.

Pastor Don Macintosh lived in southern California, though he had a serious heart condition. He got divorced from Allen's mother, **Betty Macintosh**, who left him many years ago; but he got remarried to the mother of one of Julie's classmates at Highview Academy. He died in 2007.

Peter Macintosh is married and was on Facebook but wishes to remain anonymous.

Raymond Pierce disappeared shortly after Bob Miller and Sandra Lee started dating. No further information is available.

Sandra Lee is still married to Bob Miller and they still live in southern California where Sandra taught and was a school librarian until her retirement. They had three daughters, the oldest of whom was a lesbian. Sandra and Bob are grandparents and great-grandparents. Sadly, they lost their oldest daughter in 2017 to a car accident and their middle daughter in 2020 to complications of diabetes.

Sarah remained married to her husband Ed of their teenage years; they had four children and became grandparents of six grandchildren. They still lived in Riverdale. She and Julie were in contact by email and visited once in person in the early 2000s. Sarah died on April 12, 2007, at the age of 62.

Sharon Emory grew up, married, had one child, and divorced. She still lived in southern California.

Steve Emory, as an adult, was very politically active in California and became a California State Congressperson. By profession, he became an orthodontist and practiced in southern California, where he still lives with his wife. They have two grown daughters. His parents, Dr. and Mrs. Emory, lived on The Rolling Hills Ranch on the outskirts of Riverdale where they retired. After **Dr. Emory** died on December 30, 2011, at the age of 92, **Mrs. Emory** and Julie maintained personal contact, as they had done throughout the years until Mrs. Emory's death on August 23, 2012, at the age of 92.

Victor Morgan is dead. It was Allen who told Julie in 2001, but he didn't have details. No one else knew anything about the rest of the Morgan family—until Julie found an obituary for one of his younger female siblings who "went home with the Lord on September 8, 2010." So far, no one knows whatever happened to **Gloria Martin** or Phyllis.

Don't miss out!

Visit the website below and you can sign up to receive emails whenever Juliana Harvard publishes a new book. There's no charge and no obligation.

https://books2read.com/r/B-A-EPQM-MVAPB

BOOKS 2 READ

Connecting independent readers to independent writers.

Also by Juliana Harvard

It Happened in Riverdale
It Happened in Riverdale
November Rain
That Morgan Boy
Beach City Breakup
Escape From Fate
"Marvelous"
More Riverdale Stories

About the Author

Juliana Harvard's writing spans more than five decades, from her adolescence until well past midlife. It is reflective of her most emotional moments, sometimes of ecstasy and wonder, sometimes of sadness and pain, and other times of sweet melancholy and contentment beyond words.

DISCLAIMER: "These are works of fiction. Any similarities to persons and places are frequent, intentional, and occasionally brazen, but generally fragmentary, inconsistent, and disguised with fanciful invention."

–Stephen Minot, *Three Genres*

www.ingramcontent.com/pod-product-compliance
Lightning Source LLC
Chambersburg PA
CBHW031410160726

47993CB00003B/1173